The Witch Trade

The Witch Trade

Michael Molloy

The Chicken House

An Egmont Joint Venture

For Georgia,

a friend of the elves.

First published in Great Britain in 2001
by The Chicken House
2 Palmer Street
Frome, Somerset BA11 1DS, UK

© The Chicken House 2001
© Michael Molloy 2001
Cover picture and illustrations © David Wyatt 2001

First paperback edition 2002

Michael Molloy has asserted his rights under the Copyrights, Designs and Patents
Act, 1988, to be identified as the author of this work.

British Library Cataloguing in Publication data available

ISBN 1 903434 52 1

Cover Design by David Wyatt and Mandy Sherliker
Text design by Dorchester Typesetting Group Ltd
Printed and bound in Great Britain

Contents

The Mystery of Spike and the Bird from the Sea

A bby Clover lived with her Aunt Lucy and Uncle Ben and a friend called Spike in a small seaside town called Speller, which Abby had never been able to find on a map of England.

Before her aunt and uncle had married, Ben had played the French horn in a dance band and Lucy had been a teacher in London. Now they ran the general goods store. It was just off the town square, at the head of a narrow cobbled lane that curved down to the harbour.

The shop had belonged to Abby's family for more than a hundred years. It didn't look very big from the outside, but its appearance was deceptive. Like most of the buildings in Speller, it was about the size of a cottage and was faced in whitewashed stone with bay windows that were studded with thick little panes of green glass.

Inside, there was a large room with a floor of plain oak

boards scented with spices, and a long counter with row upon row of shelves behind it. Coils of rope, old ships' lamps and every sort of tool hung from the rafters. There were stacks of barrels and boxes, lawnmowers, seed packets, tailors' dummies, bags of flower bulbs, mouse traps, rolls of cloth, sailors' knives, axes, boxes of writing paper, cans of oil, rolls of tar paper — the list was endless. No matter what item was requested in the shop, Aunt Lucy always seemed to have it somewhere.

Abby had lived above the shop ever since her parents, who were explorers, had sailed away several years before and never returned.

Before she had gone to live with her aunt and uncle, Abby's home had been in an old lighthouse that stood above the cove next to the town. When her parents had failed to return, her Aunt Lucy and Uncle Ben had rented it to a stranger whom Abby had never met.

Although her aunt and uncle loved her, Abby missed her parents with all her heart. Secretly, she hoped that despite the passing years, she would one day find them again.

Apart from Spike, who was a sea foundling, there were no other children living in Speller. But mostly, Abby was happy in the town.

Long ago, there had been other children. Abby could still remember the sound of their laughter and watching them play games when she was very small.

One spring day, when Abby's parents were away on one of their expeditions, all the children were to be taken on a sailing trip. Abby had been looking forward to it for weeks. On the morning of the treat she had stood outside the shop, impatiently hopping from one foot to another as she waited for her aunt. Suddenly, the head of a great white bird peered around the corner of the lane opposite. Then it ducked back behind the wall.

Curious, Abby had crossed the cobbles and looked up the narrow lane. The bird was waddling ahead of her. It looked back when she hesitated at the corner, and raised a wing as if it were beckoning her to follow.

Abby trotted after the bird but it always kept just ahead of her. As they reached the last house at the top of the hill, Abby could hear her Aunt Lucy calling her name and turned to look back. She could see the harbour and the town children boarding the sailing sloop that was to take them on their outing.

Abby ran down the hill as fast as she could, but it was too late. By the time she and Aunt Lucy had reached the quay, the boat was clear of the harbour.

They stood watching the boat as it seemed to get smaller and smaller. Then, quite suddenly, the great white bird Abby had followed earlier swooped down out of the sky, circled them once and flew out to sea.

'Never mind, darling,' Aunt Lucy said gently. 'We'll play some games together until the children get back.'

Abby shaded her eyes with her hand and watched the

bird, which was now a tiny white dot in the sky. 'Aunt Lucy,' she asked. 'What kind of bird was that?'

Aunt Lucy looked around her, puzzled, as there were no birds in sight. 'A seagull I suppose,' she replied.

'No,' Abby said. 'The bird that flew around us. It was much bigger than a seagull.'

'I didn't notice a big bird,' said Aunt Lucy as they turned to walk back up to the shop.

That evening, the whole town received terrible news. There had been a storm at sea and the sailing sloop had been lost with everyone aboard her. From that day, the sound of children's laughter was rarely heard in Speller.

Apart from the stranger in the lighthouse, Abby had never known anyone from the outside world to visit Speller. But, had such a person ever come, the most remarkable thing they would have noticed about the town were the gardens.

Some were like little farms, with ducks and chickens clucking and quacking in the yards. Other citizens kept cows and goats, or had pigs snorting in beds of scented hay. Speller pigs were a very special breed called 'Sweet Pinkies' because, unlike other pigs, their little huts smelled like wild heather.

Because there were so many gardens, the air was always filled with the scent of flowers. Although all the gardens were very different, the townsfolk shared curious similarities.

Tall or short, fat or thin, all the inhabitants, with the exception of Abby, Aunt Lucy, Uncle Ben and Spike, had the same ruddy complexions and deep blue eyes the colour of cornflowers.

The women always dressed in brightly coloured frocks and the men wore seamen's sweaters and tucked their trousers into sea boots, which was curious because none of them ever went to sea. The last boat in the harbour had been the sailing sloop that had taken the town's children on their final voyage.

Because nobody ever wanted to leave Speller, and the lanes were so narrow, there were no motor cars. The residents all found plenty to do in Speller.

Abby's Uncle Ben had started a town band, and Mrs Halyard ran the library over her dairy. Every Saturday night there was a dance in the Town Hall which everyone attended.

The town hall was the most important building in Speller. It was also the grandest. Made of rose-coloured red brick and trimmed with white stone, there was a short flight of steps leading to twin pillars that flanked the carved oak doors.

Abby and Spike didn't go to school. After the town folk had lost their children, the schoolhouse was turned into a grain store. As the nearest other school was far, far away, Abby and Spike took their lessons at home.

Aunt Lucy was a pretty woman with a snub nose that was dusted with freckles. She had sun-streaked hair and was slim and fit from helping Ben move the heavy barrels and boxes about the shop.

From family photographs, Abby could see how much

her mother and Aunt Lucy resembled each other, except that Aunt Lucy wore little spectacles perched on the end of her nose.

Uncle Ben was a big man with a barrel-chest and bold features. He had brown eyes and a mouth that, he claimed, was made especially wide from playing the French horn. Under his great lumpy nose flowed a fierce and magnificent handlebar moustache. When Abby was smaller, he would allow her to grasp it in her little fists so that he could lift her from the floor.

Spike was a curious looking boy, about the same age as Abby, but in complete contrast to her. Abby's hair was the colour of new chestnuts. She wore it in pigtails and had a thick fringe over her eyes. They slanted upwards and were as green as laurel leaves.

She was always brown from the sun and her cheeks red as ripe apples. Her face was a bit longer than usual, and she had her mother's snub nose. Most of the time she looked quite solemn, but when she smiled other people always smiled back.

Spike and Abby were good friends and got on better than most brothers and sisters. They spent a great deal of their time outdoors, fishing in the harbour, swimming in the next cove, or playing in the wood above the cliffs of Speller. In all their games, they were never sure who was going to win.

If one beat the other running up the cobbled lanes to the cliff-tops, or climbed a tree faster, there was always tomorrow, when the result might be quite different. They were evenly matched, except in one thing. Abby was a good swimmer, but in the sea Spike moved like a seal. It didn't matter if the water was ice cold, Spike was always in his element. And he could hold his breath for an amazing length of time.

Spike's thick mop of hair and his skin were white as snow and his eyes the palest blue, almost the colour of ice. He had pronounced cheek-bones and he always held his chin high, as if he had been trained to behave that way. He was the same height as Abby but he sometimes looked taller because he always stood up so straight.

Abby was a restless girl, so quick and curious she was seldom in the same place for long, but there was a notice-able stillness about Spike. Sometimes, when he was think-ing, it was as if he were a statue and not a boy at all.

Abby didn't care much about clothes. Her Aunt Lucy had long ago given up trying to interest her in dresses. She usually wore canvas shorts and a dark-red fisherman's smock. But Spike preferred the colour blue for his own shirts and shorts, and he never wore a jacket, no matter how cold or windy the day was.

Although Abby and Spike had only each other to play with, they seldom argued. If they did, Spike would always end the disagreement by making Abby laugh.

He rarely told jokes, but he even made adults chuckle with his dry comments — which he always delivered with a serious face.

'That boy's got a sense of humour that could make a

turtle smile,' Uncle Ben would say, and somehow the remark always made Abby feel happy. As if any praise for Spike was praise given to her as well.

The truth was, she had been lonely before Spike came to Speller and she couldn't imagine what it would be like without him.

For his part, Spike was fiercely competitive with Abby in the endless games they played. He never made the slightest allowance for her being a girl — except when they were swimming in the sea. Although he pretended indifference, he always watched her carefully in case of danger.

Uncle Ben had found Spike one morning, the year before, after a great storm. He was lying exhausted on the pebbled beach. All he wore was a swimming costume made of a strange slithery material that Uncle Ben and Aunt Lucy could not identify.

In his hand, he had clutched an object they thought was a marlin spike, used by sailors to splice ropes. It was shaped like a short stubby poker but made of very hard wood.

Uncle Ben had wrapped Spike in a piece of tarpaulin and carried him back to the store. He lay in a deep sleep for two days. At first they weren't sure what to do with him, then Aunt Lucy decided he would be better off if he stayed with her.

At first, while he slept, he had sometimes talked in a strange language. It sounded like clicks and whistles. And all the time he clutched the old marlin spike tightly in his hand. Uncle Ben had tried to take it from him but he wouldn't let it go. 'That's why we called him Spike,' Uncle Ben always said whenever he told the story.

When Spike did eventually wake up, he did not speak again in the language they had heard him muttering in his sleep, and he could remember nothing about his life before coming to Speller.

Aunt Lucy said he was clever and quick to learn, but his real passion was swimming. He and Abby swam every day, regardless of the weather.

They always headed for a cove set in the high cliffs that flanked the town. Above the cove stood the old lighthouse where Abby had once lived. Recently, she had noticed that the stranger, who now rented it, was often watching them from the balcony.

She had never seen the stranger near the town and had meant to ask Aunt Lucy about him but, somehow, it kept slipping her mind.

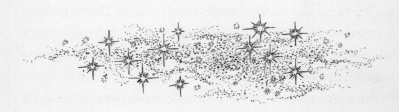

The Stranger in the Lighthouse

One blustery November afternoon after they had been swimming, Abby and Spike were climbing the path up from the cove. Usually the weather around Speller was good, but today the sky was dark and a thunderstorm had broken as they reached the top of the cliffs. Abby was looking up at the darting streaks of lightning when she slipped and turned her ankle.

She tried to hop but the pain was too much for her and she had to sit down. She was about to send Spike for help when the stranger from the lighthouse appeared at the top of the cliffs.

'Hold on,' he called out in a deep voice. He scrambled down the path and scooped Abby up in his arms. He was a tall, gaunt man, with a shock of iron-grey hair that showed beneath his captain's cap. A seaman's pea jacket with brass buttons and a soft, grey wool fisherman's sweater hung on his bony frame. His grey cord trousers were tucked into high, black leather sea boots.

His long narrow face was as dark and seamed as an old oak plank, so that his teeth looked very white when he smiled at Abby. Black bushy eyebrows jutted above his big hooked nose and a thin white scar curved down from his left cheek to end under his jaw.

Spike followed the stranger as he carried Abby through the pouring rain to the entrance of the lighthouse. 'Step lively boy and open the door for me,' the man said in a gruff voice.

Spike looked uncertain and the man spoke again — this time in the strange language of clicks and whistles that Spike had once used. Spike smiled and immediately did what he was asked.

They entered the lighthouse and Abby remembered the great iron spiral staircase that led upwards to where the light had once been. The tall man carried her effortlessly to the top of the stairs and they entered a wide circular room that was now furnished like a ship's cabin.

There was a hammock, several great sea chests bound with brass, old sailing instruments, harpoons, a collection of ships in bottles and one mighty chair made from gnarled driftwood that had been smoothed by the sea. Ancient charts of the oceans of the world covered the stone walls. The man sat Abby on one of the chests and asked, 'Which ankle did you hurt, girl?'

Abby extended her left foot and the man held the swollen ankle in both of his hands. They were hard and rough but surprisingly warm. After a moment she felt the pain recede.

'Try that now,' he instructed and Abby stood up. The ankle felt as good as new.

'Thank you very much, Mr – ?' she said.

'Starlight, Captain Adam Starlight – of Bright Town,' he answered.

'Where is Bright Town?' Spike asked.

'It doesn't exist any more,' he answered briskly. 'It used to be in New England.'

'New England! That's in America, isn't it?' said Abby.

'It surely is. And what may your name be, young lady?'

'Abigail Clover, but everyone calls me Abby.'

'Well, I'm very pleased to meet you,' he said with a sudden smile.

A flash of lightning lit up the room and a particularly loud peal of thunder seemed to shake the foundations of the lighthouse. The lightning flash had reflected on the gleaming blades of the harpoons hanging on the wall.

'Do you hunt whales with those?' Abby asked when the sound of thunder had died away.

'No,' Starlight answered. 'I take them away from whale hunters.'

Abby was interested to know more about the captain, but she was concerned that she and Spike would be late home.

'Thank you for your hospitality, Captain, but I think we'd better go now,' she said. 'My Aunt Lucy is expecting us.'

'Best to wait a while,' Captain Starlight replied easily. 'The storm is right overhead, it will pass soon.'

'I like storms,' said Spike who was examining a rack of marlin spikes set against the rough stone wall. 'It makes swimming more fun.'

Starlight turned to him. 'So storms don't bother you, lad?'

Spike nodded. 'They don't bother the whales either, and they're much bigger than I am.' He continued to examine the marlin spikes and was now taking them from the rack one by one.

Captain Starlight asked him, 'Why are you doing that, lad?'

Spike looked up. 'I'm trying to see if they're like mine,' he answered.

The captain looked thoughtful. 'You don't look as if you come from these parts.'

'He doesn't,' Abby answered. 'My Uncle Ben found him on the beach and all he had was his marlin spike and his swimming costume.' Abby took the costume from Spike and held it out to the captain. 'Look, it's made of strange stuff.'

Captain Starlight took the costume from her and examined it carefully before handing it back.

'Perhaps you could bring your spike to show me sometime,' Starlight suggested.

'I can bring it tomorrow, maybe,' Spike replied.

'We shall have to ask my Aunt Lucy if we can come,' Abby said.

Starlight nodded. He thought for a moment and then said to her, 'How old are you now, Abby? I seem to have forgotten.'

'There's no reason you should have known my age,' Abby answered.

Captain Starlight smiled again and nodded. 'Quite right, but can you whistle yet?'

'Of course I can,' Abby said.

'Lots of girls can't.'

'Well I can, just listen,' and she whistled the first part of a tune that was a particular favourite of the town band.

The captain studied her for a moment as if he was making up his mind about something, then he went to one of the sea chests and found a large leather bag that looked empty.

He took out a pinch of what seemed to be silver dust and placed it carefully in the palm of his hand. Then he sprinkled it over Abby's head. Abby felt dizzy for a moment and she shivered, feeling as if tiny charges of electricity were tingling all over her body.

'What did you do?' she asked.

'Don't worry,' the captain answered. 'It won't harm you.'

'But will it do me any good?' Abby replied, sounding rather like her Aunt Lucy.

'We'll see. Can you can repeat this tune after me?' He whistled a few notes of a strange, fluting melody. It was unlike anything Abby had ever heard.

'Can you manage that?' he asked.

'I think so,' Abby said.

'Come and stand here while you do,' the captain said, and he positioned himself before a dim old mirror. As she whistled the tune, Abby watched their reflections in the dark glass. To her astonishment, just as she finished the last note, her own reflection vanished and all she could see was the figure of Captain Starlight.

'Where have I gone?' Abby called out, astonished.

'Don't worry,' Starlight replied. 'You're still there. Take hold of my hand.' She reached out and could feel his grip but she was still completely invisible.

'How do I come back?' she asked nervously.

'Whistle the tune backwards.' Starlight instructed.

'I'm not sure if I can remember,' replied Abby, worried. 'Will I stay invisible for ever?'

'Copy me,' said the captain, and he whistled the tune in reverse.

Abby did so and, to her relief, her reflection returned.

'That's good,' said Spike. 'I thought for a moment you might be invisible for ever. People would have thought I was going around talking to myself when I was with you.'

Abby gave him what Aunt Lucy called one her old-fashioned looks. 'I prefer it when you make jokes about other people, Spike,' she said.

'Most people do,' said Spike, sighing.

Abby looked back at Starlight. He smiled at her. 'You managed that very well.'

'Will I always be able to do it?' Abby asked.

'As long as you remember the tune,' Starlight said. 'And as long as you never use it to do anything bad.'

'I'll remember.'

'I hope so,' Starlight said, a little sadly. 'People forget a lot as they grow older.'

Abby looked out of the window again. The storm had passed and a new moon reflected on the calm surface of the sea. 'We'd better get home, Spike,' she said, still finding it difficult to believe she could vanish at will. She had begun to wonder if she were dreaming.

'You'd better take one of my lanterns,' the captain said. 'It will be dark on the cliffs.'

He opened a sea chest, took out a ball made of thick green glass, and handed it to Abby. It was the float from a fisherman's net.

'How does it work?' she asked doubtfully.

'Your hand will warm it up in a moment,' Captain Starlight answered and, as he spoke, a glow inside the globe grew brighter until it lit up the room. The glass surface remained quite cool.

'What makes it do that?' Abby asked.

'I filled it with St Elmo's fire,' the captain answered. 'Don't worry, it's quite safe.'

He took them to the door of the lighthouse. 'Oh, one more thing,' he said, handing Abby a seashell the size of her hand. 'If you want to talk to me just speak into this.'

Abby glanced at it. The shell looked quite ordinary, but she put it in her pocket.

'See you in the morning,' Spike called out as they set off home along the cliffs.

'Ring the bell hard,' the captain answered. 'I may take a little time to come to the door.'

When they reached home, Aunt Lucy had just started to worry about them.

'We stopped to talk to the man in the lighthouse,' Abby explained.

'Adam Starlight?' said Aunt Lucy.

'Yes, how did you come to know him?'

'He was a friend of your mother and father, darling,' Aunt Lucy said, as she served them up their supper.

Abby had intended to tell her aunt and uncle that Captain Starlight had taught her how to make herself invisible, but somehow she knew it wasn't yet the right time. After supper, she went straight up to bed. She had a lot to think about. Spike had gone to bed as well. He slept in the room next to Abby's, and always went to sleep the moment he closed his eyes.

Abby lay with the shell Starlight had given her on the pillow beside her. The light was out and through the open window she could hear the sound of the sea and the soft tones of Uncle Ben practising on his French horn below.

It was a cold night but she was warm under her covers. There was just enough light from the moon to see the glass globe the captain had given her. It looked like an ordinary fisherman's float now the fire inside it had faded. 'Perhaps I imagined it all,' she murmured.

In answer, the captain's voice spoke to her through the shell as clearly as if he were there in the room.

'Pick up the ball, Abby,' he told her. 'And just think how much light you want.'

She slipped out of bed and picked up the ball. 'A good candle's worth,' she thought. Slowly, the ball began to glow, but this time not half so brightly.

As she climbed back into bed, another question occurred to her. 'If I became invisible and so did my clothes, why didn't everything vanish, the earth beneath my feet — in fact, the whole world?' she asked.

'Only your immediate things vanish, such as your clothes,' the captain answered. 'But with practice you will be able to hold quite big things and they will vanish too. It may take a little time to learn though.'

Suddenly, Abby began to feel very tired. 'Goodnight, Captain Starlight,' she said.

'Goodnight, Abby,' the captain's voice answered softly.

The Secret Lagoon

'Did you remember to bring your marlin spike?' Abby asked as she and Spike walked along the cliff-top to the lighthouse the following morning.

'Of course I did,' Spike answered, lifting his shirt to show the length of wood tucked in his belt.

The weather had stayed fair since the previous night. There was a sharp easterly wind blowing and sunshine sparkled on the incoming tide.

'I wouldn't mind a swim first,' Spike said wistfully, as they reached the lighthouse.

'After we've seen the captain,' Abby said firmly.

'The sea looks perfect — nice and cold,' Spike said as he rang the ship's bell which hung by the door.

'It always looks perfect to you, Spike,' Abby answered. 'Sometimes I wonder if you're not part fish.'

'I wouldn't mind being a dolphin,' he replied. 'They have the most fun.'

They waited quite a few minutes but the captain did not come to the door.

'Perhaps he's gone for a walk,' Spike said. 'Shall we come back after we've had a swim?'

'Stay here,' Abby said sternly. 'He said he might take some time to answer the door. He's probably at the top of the tower.' Abby rang the bell again. Eventually, there was a sound from inside the lighthouse and the door swung open.

'Come in,' the captain said cheerfully. 'Sorry to keep you waiting. Did you bring the marlin spike?'

'Uncle Ben says it's probably from a windjammer,' Spike said as he handed it over.

Captain Starlight nodded. 'It's made to *look* as if it's from a windjammer,' he replied. 'But really it's from something quite different.' He gave the knob at the end a sharp twist and, like a sword drawn from a scabbard, a long carved key emerged from the shaft.

'How did you know that would happen?' Abby asked.

'I've been looking for this for quite a while,' the captain answered softly.

'What does it do?' Spike said.

'Come with me and I'll show you,' Starlight replied.

He led them to a large trapdoor with great iron hinges, set into the floor behind the spiral staircase. He inserted the key in the lock and with a mighty effort lifted the trapdoor.

'So that's what it's for,' Abby said.

'Oh, it does a sight more than that,' Starlight replied.

Abby peered into the darkness below. She could see the top of a wide flight of steps leading down into the cliff.

'Follow me,' Starlight said, taking a lantern from the wall. He led them down the narrow steps carved into the chalk beneath them.

Just as Abby judged they should be getting quite close to the level of the sea, the stairs stopped and they found themselves in a wide passage. It twisted and turned for a time until they suddenly emerged in a cavern so vast it could have held the entire town of Speller under its mighty roof.

'Well, here's a surprise, and no denying,' Starlight said softly as they gazed about. A great lagoon stretched out before them and it contained an extraordinary sight. An armada of sailing ships packed the water. There were schooners and cutters, tea clippers, Chinese junks and galleys from the Mediterranean, Arabian dhows and New England merchantmen. There were fat Dutch coastal boats and Thames sailing barges. It was a vast fleet with sails furled, resting on still water in the silence of the massive cavern.

Abby's gaze darted from ship to ship, half expecting to see some ghostly sailor still aboard. Her eyes finally came to rest on one smaller boat, anchored quite close to them in the dark water. It was very different to the others. There were no masts and the little craft glowed with a soft bluish light which, Abby now saw, illuminated the entire cavern.

Abby looked around her and was puzzled. There was no entrance to the lagoon. She could not see how any of the craft could have entered the cavern from the open sea that lay beyond the great rock wall.

the soft, blue light she looked again at the strange lit-
raft that had caught her attention. It was as sleek and
shapely as a racing yacht but, instead of a hull and deck
made of wood or metal, the boat seemed to be clad in silvery scales, like a giant fish.

The cabin, set halfway along the deck, was in the shape
of a giant turtle's shell. It looked to Abby as though it had
grown into its elegant form rather than been shaped by
craftsmen. On closer inspection, she could see that it had
been made with extraordinary skill, and she marvelled at
the beautiful carving and its graceful flowing lines.

'Did you know the lagoon was here, Captain?' Abby asked.

Starlight shook his head. 'No, but I've seen this beauty
before,' he said, nodding towards the little boat.

'How much room is there aboard?' Spike asked.

'She'll take a crew of seven at a pinch,' Captain Starlight
replied. 'But one person can handle her – if they know
what they're doing.'

Starlight stepped aboard and gestured for Spike and
Abby to follow him. He inserted the same key and opened
a hatchway in the cabin shell. Once inside, Abby looked
about her in wonder. Soft light glowed from the walls of
the cabin but she could see no actual source.

The bulkheads were lined with polished wood and
finished in silvery metal. There were deep comfortable
seats upholstered in a green velvety material arranged
around a chart table. Set in the centre of the table was a
great crystal ball. Abby saw there was another one set
above the steering wheel.

Starlight sat in a captain's chair and inserted Spike's key
in a control panel. Immediately a row of dials with strange
symbols glowed with light above the large crystal. 'What
kind of engine does it have, Captain?' Spike asked.

'*She*, lad,' the captain corrected him. 'Everything
that floats on water is a she. Remember that. She has
salt engines.'

'Salt engines?' Abby echoed in astonishment.

'Very advanced principle,' Starlight said. 'They suck in
sea water and extract the salt which the converters burn to
fuel the jets. Lovely bit of design. It also means we have a
constant supply of fresh water — so there's no need for salty
showers at sea.'

'I've never heard of engines that run on salt,' said Abby.
'They must be very modern.'

Starlight chuckled. 'Ten thousand years old, give or
take a few centuries.'

'Ten thousand years!' Abby gasped.

Captain Starlight turned to look at her. 'This is an Atlantis Boat, Abby. The Atlanteans knew a thing or two about marine engineering.'

'Wow! Do you mean the lost continent of Atlantis?' Abby asked. Aunt Lucy had told them about the legend in their lessons.

'That's the place,' said the captain. 'Although Atlantis was never really lost, you know.' He turned back to the control panel. 'Now this old girl hasn't been out in a long time. Let's give her a sea trial.'

'How will you get through the rock?' asked Spike. 'There's no way out to the sea.'

'Let's try this,' the captain answered as he pressed a button on the control panel. There was a long booming note that sounded like a whale sighing.

The great rock face ahead of them slowly began to rise. The cavern filled with daylight and as their eyes adjusted they saw the open sea beyond.

Captain Starlight pulled a lever and a sudden throb of power shuddered gently throughout the craft, then settled into a low humming sound. He pulled the throttle lever down several notches. The boat quivered for a moment, then surged forward at alarming speed.

They shot out of the cavern and into the open sea. The boat hurtled across the bay leaving a cloud of squawking seagulls in its wake.

'Sorry about that,' said Starlight, easing back on the

throttle. 'I'm a bit rusty.' The boat now came to a standstill and bobbed gently on the waves of the incoming tide.

Abby's head filled with questions. 'How did you know the boat was here? When did you see it last? Who made the cavern?' she asked.

'I'll tell you soon,' Starlight answered. 'I just want to try something else.' He studied the glowing instruments briefly before taking the controls again.

This time, Spike and Abby both drew in a sharp breath as the boat dived beneath the waves!

'We've sunk, Captain,' said Spike, sounding calm. 'Did you jettison the plug?'

'No need to worry, lad,' replied Starlight. 'Everything's under control.'

'Oh, I'm not worried,' said Spike. 'I'm used to being under water. I was only concerned for you and Abby.'

Starlight manipulated the controls again and the beams of powerful searchlights lit up the waters around them. The boat surged forward, and Abby felt as if she were inside a gigantic aquarium. Tangles of weeds grew from the sandy sea bed and shoals of fish flickered past as the magical boat sped along.

When they came to the wreck of an old sailing ship that lay half buried in the sand, Starlight slowed the boat down.

'Perhaps there's treasure aboard,' said Abby.

'No, there's just a family of lobsters living in it,' said Spike. 'I know these waters pretty well.'

'Time to get back,' said Starlight. He raised the boat to

the surface and steered towards the cliffs below the light-house. When they were back inside the cavern, Captain Starlight sounded the booming signal and the cliff descended to seal off the secret lagoon.

The Secret of the Atlantis Boat

Captain Starlight still hadn't given Abby and Spike an explanation for the mysterious little boat. As soon as they returned to his quarters in the lighthouse, he had disappeared into the galley, leaving them bursting with curiosity.

Finally, he came back with a heaped tray. 'There's coffee for me, and hot chocolate and home-made biscuits for you two,' he said. 'But don't touch the fish cakes, they're for Benbow.'

Abby and Spike looked at one another in surprise. There was no one else in the room.

The captain opened a window and gave a long piercing whistle. A few moments later there was the sound of beating wings as a great white seabird landed on the sill and peered inquisitively at Spike and Abby. A memory stirred in Abby's mind as the great bird hopped into the room.

Benbow settled on a chest near the table. At a nod from the captain, he began to peck delicately at one of the fishcakes on the tray.

'Is he tame?' Spike asked, looking a trifle nervously at the powerful beak so close to his elbow.

'No, he's not tame,' the captain answered. 'But there's no need to worry, he's no danger to you. He's an albatross. Some people believe they can foretell the future.'

'Will you tell us about the cavern now, Captain?' Abby asked.

He took a long swallow from his mug of coffee and sat back in his chair. 'Let me tell you a story first. Do you know how the town of Speller got its name?' Both Abby and Spike shook their heads. The captain began. 'Long ago, Speller was a busy port used by the Sea Witches.'

'I thought witches were just in fairy stories,' said Abby doubtfully.

The captain shook his head. 'Oh, no,' he said. 'There's always been real witches, good ones and bad ones; and what's more, they've been battling each other for ever.'

'What were Sea Witches?' Spike asked.

'*Are* Sea Witches, lad,' Starlight said, correcting him. 'They still exist, although they don't go to sea any more. Sea Witches used to control the supply of Ice Dust. That's why it was called the Witch Trade.'

Abby was dubious. Despite the extraordinary things that had happened in the last few days, she still half expected there to be an ordinary explanation for the mysteries she had experienced.

'And where are the Sea Witches now?' she asked. 'I've

never seen any in Speller.'

Starlight gave a little laugh. 'Oh, yes you have, Abby. That's what the townsfolk are.'

Abby shook her head. 'I don't mean to be rude, Captain Starlight, but I've lived in Speller all my life and I've never seen anyone go to sea since the day the children were lost. Never mind being a witch.'

The captain paused and then said, 'Would you believe your mother and father if they told you the same story?'

'I don't think my parents believed in magic,' Abby said softly.

'Oh, yes they did,' said the captain. As he spoke he rose from his chair and took a letter from one of his chests. He handed it to Abby. All that was written on it was the name *Captain Adam Starlight* in her father's handwriting. Abby recognized it immediately as Aunt Lucy had shown her his old letters many times. She opened the folded sheets of paper and began to read aloud to Spike.

'Dear Adam

'Good news! We think we've found another source of Ice Dust somewhere near Antarctica.

'When you left us to go home to Bright Town, Madge and I discovered a hoard of old maps and documents aboard the Atlantis Boat. Actually, they were copies, but there was also a strange note saying the originals had been given for safe keeping to Polartius — whoever that may be!

'One of the documents was the translation of an Icelandic saga, complete with maps. It told of a land beneath Antarctica where

there were vast deposits of magic white powder! We think it must be Ice Dust. We had a fairly good look at the map but then Nettlebed, the deck-hand, accidentally dropped the container of documents overboard.

'He must have been upset by the accident because he took off after that and we never saw him again. Madge and I could remember quite a bit of the map, so we decided to return to Speller in the Atlantis Boat and fit out a bigger ship to look for the Ice Dust.

'When we returned to Speller we found a very bad state of affairs. Benbow's premonition was correct. The children are all gone — except for Abby. Somehow, Benbow managed to save her. The Sea Witches believe their children were lost in a storm, but we suspect the Night Witches may have kidnapped them to use as slaves.

'The Night Witch raids are becoming more ferocious. They are destroying all the ships of the Sea Witches, who have no weapons they can use against the Shark Boats. Since no supplies of Ice Dust are getting through to the Light Witches any more, the Night Witches are becoming more and more powerful.

'If we can find just one big cargo of Ice Dust it may be enough to enable the Light Witches to fight back. I have taken the key to the Atlantis Boat with me and hidden the boat itself along with the Sea Witch fleet.

'The Night Witches won't attack Speller because, over the years, the whole town became impregnated with Ice Dust. In the days when it was plentiful, the Sea Witches used to mix it in with the whitewash on the houses for good luck.

'If all goes well, we should be back in a few months with a

cargo. Meanwhile, we have left Abby with Madge's sister Lucy.

'I left this letter with your London bank because I have no idea where in the world you may be at the moment, but I know you will eventually check there, some time in the future.

Your friends

Harry and Madge Clover.'

Abby looked at Benbow. Now she had remembered where she'd seen the great bird before. 'So it was Benbow I followed the day the children were lost. I thought he looked familiar!' she exclaimed.

'That's right,' Captain Starlight replied. 'At that time I was with your parents, far away, but Benbow told me something bad was going to happen and he flew off to save you.'

'You can talk to Benbow?' Spike asked.

The captain nodded. 'I suppose so, in a way. But it's more like we can understand each other's thoughts.'

Abby put down the letter. 'I'm getting rather confused, Captain. Please can you explain all this from the beginning?'

The captain took another sip from his cup of coffee and began.

'First of all, you've got to understand about witches. For the past thousand years or so, things went pretty well for the Light Witches because they had the Ice Dust. Pure Ice Dust is deadly to Night Witches. It's too clean for them, you see.'

Abby and Spike nodded.

'The Night Witches had to use inferior stuff they called Dirt Dust for their spells. They manufacture it from the sweepings of haunted houses, the bottoms of dustbins and the black stuff from under the fingernails of bad people.'

Spike and Abby nodded again.

'The Light Witches had trouble with the Night Witches from time to time. It was never anything they couldn't handle because the Light Witches had plentiful supplies of Ice Dust.'

'So, what exactly is Ice Dust?' Abby wanted to know.

'No one is quite sure. You can't make it. It's only found where the water is totally pure and very cold. And it's the stuff of which all good spells are made.

But then, not too long ago, the Night Witches made a terrible discovery. They found a way of mixing Ice Dust with something new they had invented. They took Dirt Dust and combined it with all sorts of toxic waste, added sewer water and finally crushed it. They called the result Black Dust.'

Starlight could see that Abby and Spike were intensely interested, so he continued.

'With Black Dust they could now make more powerful spells. But they still couldn't handle the Ice Dust without endangering themselves. The Night Witches who were making the Black Dust were all dying. So they needed slaves to mix it for them. That's why they kidnapped the children of Speller.'

'Why didn't the Light Witches fight back?'

'They tried to but it was too late. Unfortunately, the Light Witches tended to be a bit old-fashioned. They liked to keep things as they were. And the Sea Witches are worse. They even preferred to carry on the Ice Dust trade with wooden sailing ships.'

Abby was confused again. 'What is the difference between Light Witches and Sea Witches?'

'Light Witches may be old-fashioned, but they like to be out and about in the world. They do all sorts of jobs. Some of them are quite famous.'

'What about Sea Witches?' Spike wanted to know.

Starlight handed another fish cake to Benbow before he answered.

'Sea Witches are different. They don't want to live in the outside world. They like to be with their own folk. Because they love the sea so much, they gave up almost everything else. They even stopped learning to make spells, except for a few that were handy at sea.'

'Such as?' Spike prompted.

'Sea Witches can summon their own winds, so their ships are never becalmed. They can make rain as well, so they always have fresh water at sea. And they always know exactly where they are on the oceans of the world.'

'And the Sea Witches now live only in Speller?' Abby asked.

'They do now,' Starlight said, suddenly looking very sad. 'They also used to live in a place called Bright Town, in America where I come from.'

'What happened?' Abby asked.

'The Night Witches used Black Dust to build a fleet of fearsome raiding ships which they called Shark Boats. They drove the Sea Witches from the seas and they destroyed my hometown. Then they took over the Ice Dust trade for themselves. You see, they need an incredibly large amount of Ice Dust to make Black Dust. The last I heard, the deposits in the Arctic were almost exhausted. But as you saw in your father's letter, Abby, he thought he had located a new source.'

Abby was still bubbling with more questions. 'What about my parents, and Aunt Lucy and Uncle Ben,' she said. 'They're not witches, are they?'

Starlight shook his head. 'No, Abby, but your ancestors have been friends to the Sea Witches for generations. Did you know your mother's family name was Elvin?'

Abby nodded.

'Well, Elvin means friend of the elves; and elves are very close to Light Witches. Your ancestor, Jack Elvin was invited to come to Speller to open the shop. One of the conditions for becoming a Sea Witch was that they couldn't become involved in anything to do with making money, or they lost the right to carry out the Witch Trade. That's why they needed an outsider to run the shop, and do all sorts of other things around the town. I think it was him who built the Town Hall.'

'Are you a Light Witch, Captain Starlight?' asked Spike.

'No, lad,' he replied. 'My family designed ships for the Light Witches many years ago, in Bright Town.'

'But you can make spells?'

'I have *some* powers because I've been around Light Witches for so long.'

'How did my mother and father get so involved in all of this if they're not Sea Witches?' Abby asked.

'Your mother knew all about the Witch Trade,' said Starlight. 'After all, she grew up in Speller. Your father was an outsider, like your Uncle Ben, and met your mother at college. She told him everything when he asked her to marry him.'

'Why did nobody tell me?' Abby asked.

'Your Aunt Lucy was going to tell you on your next birthday.'

'How do you know that?'

'I know a lot about you, Abby. Your parents told me all about you when they hired my ship to go exploring. That's when we discovered the secret of Atlantis.'

'You discovered Atlantis?'

Starlight shook his head. 'No, we discovered the *secret* of Atlantis.'

He went to one of the charts on the wall and pointed to a place near Bermuda in the Atlantic Ocean. 'It was here. We found it when your parents charted my boat. Your father first contacted me after he'd read a book called *Lost Secrets of the Seven Seas*. I was mentioned in it.'

'How did he contact you?'

'He dreamed about me.'

'How did you know?'

'Benbow told me. The albatross is a very mysterious bird. So I got in touch with your father. He wanted my help to search for something.'

'What was it?'

Starlight put down his coffee. 'The answer to a riddle in an old sea shanty the Sea Witches used to sing when they were at sea. Your father thought it contained a special secret.'

'How did it go?' Spike asked.

Starlight began to sing:

> *'There is an Island where none should be*
> *Shaped like a fish-hook set in the sea*
> *South-by-west lies a Spanish treasure*
> *Lying on wealth you cannot measure*
> *If your heart be kind and true*
> *A door will open just for you*
> *But if your heart is dark and cruel*

You'll lie with the fishes, like a fool.'

When he'd finished, he tapped the chart again and Abby looked to where his finger pointed. It was the island of Bermuda, and it was shaped just like a fish-hook.

'We set sail for Bermuda in *Ishmael*, my boat. Your mother, your father, me and a deckhand called Nettlebed whom I'd taken on for the voyage. The island of Bermuda has always been a mystery,' Starlight continued. 'Sailors used to say there shouldn't be land there at all. So we followed the song and started exploring wrecks south-by-west of the Island. One day, when they were diving around a Spanish galleon, your mother and father discovered the Time Bubble.'

'Time Bubble?' Abby and Spike echoed in unison.

Starlight nodded as he poured himself more coffee. 'It was the day after a storm. The rough sea had shifted the sand on the bottom quite a bit. Nettlebed was on deck and your parents and I were in the water. When we got down to where the galleon lay, we saw that the storm had cleared the sand from under her and she was lying on a great smooth dome. It was too perfect to be a rock.

'As your parents got closer a whirlpool seemed to come out of it. They were drawn down and all the turbulence churned the sand up into the sea. I couldn't see more than a few feet ahead of me. I was further away and the current kept me away from the swirling drag. I thought your parents were finished, Abby.

'The whirlpool stopped and, when the sand had settled,

all I could see was the wreck of the Spanish galleon. I stayed down until my air started to give out, then I had to get back to my boat. I went down three more times but there was no sign of them.

'Finally, that evening when Nettlebed and I were packing up to go home, your parents suddenly returned. They were in the Atlantis Boat and had all sorts of extraordinary things they'd found aboard.'

'What sort of things?' asked Spike.

'Gadgets, inventions. Bits and pieces the like of which we'd never seen before. There were clothes that altered to fit the shape of your body and stayed dry and warm no matter how cold and wet they became.'

'What else?' Spike asked.

'A telescope that could see beyond the horizon. It also let you hear what people were saying, even though they were miles away. A magnet that made things weigh less. Tools that could melt away stone and cut metal like scissors through paper. I guess that's how your father made the great cavern for the Sea Witch fleet, Abby.'

Abby had grown quiet. 'So, if Spike had the key to the Atlantis Boat, he must have been given it by my parents, because they took it with them on their last voyage.'

Starlight nodded. 'That's right.'

'And I can't remember anything about it,' Spike said gloomily.

'We know they were going to Antarctica,' Starlight answered. 'And now we know they may still be alive. But they must be somewhere pretty bad.'

'Why do you say that?' Abby asked.

Starlight spoke carefully. 'I've sent Benbow out many times to try to find them. He's had no luck. Some powerful dark force must keep them prisoner if Benbow can't locate them.'

Abby didn't want to think about that. She quickly changed the subject. 'Was there anything else on the boat?' she asked.

'A little statue that could speak.'

'What happened to it?' Spike asked.

'I've still got it,' Starlight said. 'I kept one or two things.' He went to a chest and took out a model about 50 centimetres high. It was of a boy and a girl riding a dolphin, carved out of dull grey stone. He placed it before them on a chest. As they gazed at it, the statue rose slowly into the air and the stone suddenly took on the appearance of living creatures!

The little boy and girl waved from the back of the dolphin and then Abby could hear Spike's special language.

'Speak to it in English,' Starlight said.

'Hello,' Abby said. 'My name is Abby Clover. I'm from Speller.'

The voice spoke again and said, 'Hello, Abby.' Another shimmering image formed in the air above the statue. It showed a cluster of silvery white buildings on a mountainside that ran down to a dark blue sea.

Abby recognised the shapes from the pictures in a book that Aunt Lucy used to teach them history. They looked like ancient Greek buildings.

'Greetings to those who find this record of our visit to your world,' the voice said. 'What you see before you is the city of Atlantis.'

As the voice spoke, Abby, Spike and the captain watched the buildings of the city rise slowly into the air and reassemble themselves before the voice began again.

'This is the starship in which we journey. Atlantis has long gone from your part of the universe. But we have left you a pleasure craft and a few of our toys. You may find them useful, but be warned, they will do those who are bad at heart no good at all. Goodbye to you for now. We shall meet again when you begin your long journey to the stars.'

The voice stopped and the life seemed to go out of the statue. It sank back on to the chest.

Starlight turned to Abby and Spike, who were still staring in wonderment at the stone object. 'So, that's how we discovered the secret of Atlantis. The popular legend was wrong. Atlantis didn't sink beneath the sea, it flew away to visit other stars.'

'What happened next?' asked Abby. 'Why did you suddenly leave for Bright Town?'

'I received a warning from Benbow that it was under attack from the Night Witches. By the time I got there, the Night Witches had done their evil work. Bright Town was completely destroyed and all its people killed. But I knew where they had hidden their own store of Ice Dust.

I took it and ever since I have been hunting the Night Witches' Shark Boats and destroying them with harpoons coated with Ice Dust.

'The last of my Ice Dust is almost gone, so I came to England to search for your parents. They weren't in Speller but I found the letter at my bank in London. Then I came back here to see if I could locate the cavern, and maybe even start the Atlantis Boat. Luckily I found Spike – and the key.'

Abby suddenly realised there was something this mysterious man hadn't yet told them. She stood up and asked, 'Who are you really, Captain Starlight?'

'I thought you would have guessed by now, Abby. I am the Ancient Mariner.'

'The Ancient Mariner…' Spike repeated in a strange voice – and fainted.

Captain Starlight
Plans an Expedition

When Spike recovered from his faint, he found himself lying in Captain Starlight's hammock with a large Dover sole flapping on his forehead. It felt very cool. Abby had resumed questioning Captain Starlight.

'I thought the Ancient Mariner was just a legend,' he heard her say.

'I am a legend,' Starlight replied. 'But I exist as well. Such a thing is possible, you know.'

Abby wracked her brains for a moment. 'But doesn't the legend say that the Ancient Mariner was cursed because he shot an albatross?'

Starlight folded his arms.

'That's just a lot of nonsense put about by the Night Witches. They even got someone to write a poem — all rubbish.' He held out an arm and Benbow hopped over and sat on it. 'Would Benbow do that if I were someone who'd shot one of his relatives?'

'So what is the truth?' Abby persisted. 'The legend also says you're hundreds of years old.'

'That part is true,' he replied. 'I was such a good ship-builder, the Sea Witches in Bright Town wanted me to go on living for ever.'

Spike stirred and Starlight turned to him. 'He's all right now, Benbow,' he said. 'You can put the fish back in the sea.'

Benbow hopped over to Spike, delicately removed the flapping fish from his brow and flew out of the window.

'How are you feeling, Spike?' Abby asked anxiously.

'Fine,' Spike replied, sitting up.

'Do you know why you fainted?' Abby asked.

'It was the shock of what Captain Starlight said. "Find the Ancient Mariner." That's what they told me to do.'

'Who told you?' Abby asked.

'I'm not absolutely sure, but I think it was your mother and father, Abby!'

'So they *could* still be alive!' she said excitedly. 'Can you remember anything else, Spike?'

He thought for a moment, then shook his head. 'I can't even remember what they looked like. All I can recall are the words, "Find the Ancient Mariner".'

'And what about your own mother and father? Do you remember who they are?' Abby asked.

'No,' he answered. 'I know I escaped from somewhere by swimming.' Spike said slowly. 'There was a narrow crack in the rock, just wide enough for me to slip through under-water. That's all.'

'How are we going to find my parents?' Abby said, crestfallen.

'There must be another map,' Starlight said with sudden conviction.

'How can you be sure?' said Abby.

'Because the Night Witches must have found one that showed the deposits in Antarctica. It will be in their head-quarters.'

'Would they keep it there?' Spike asked.

Starlight nodded. 'The Night Witches keep all their tro-phies. They like to boast about them.'

'How shall we get it?' Abby asked.

'We'll have to steal it from them,' Captain Starlight replied, and they could hear the determination in his voice. Turning to Spike, he said, 'How are you feeling now, lad?'

'Fine,' Spike answered, swinging down from the hammock.

The captain opened another of his chests and produced two large items of clothing and handed them to Spike and Abby.

Abby could feel that hers was as soft and light as one of her Aunt Lucy's silk handkerchiefs. She held it up and saw it was a long, dark blue coat that was baggy enough to cover a large man. There was also a hood attached.

'They're far too big for us,' Abby said.

'They're Atlantis capes. Put them on,' the captain replied.

As they did so, the coats suddenly contracted. They wound around Spike and Abby's legs and even covered their feet. The material felt wonderfully warm.

'If you pull the hood over your face, you can see through the weave, and you will still be able to breathe. That's all you'll need,' Starlight said. 'The boat will provide the rest.'

'What are we going to do now?' Abby asked.

The captain had taken a large kit bag and was filling it rapidly from the contents of various chests as he answered. Then he took down the largest harpoon hanging on the wall.

'First, we're going to tell your Uncle Ben and Aunt Lucy that we're off on a trip, then we're going to London to steal the map, then we're sailing to Antarctica to rescue your parents.'

'That's a lot to do on a Sunday,' Spike said thoughtfully.

Aboard the Ishmael

Captain Starlight stood with Abby and Spike and rapped on the shop's brass knocker. When the door opened, he raised his cap and said, 'Hello, Lucy, good to see you again.'

'So, Adam Starlight, you've called at last,' Aunt Lucy replied. 'You'd better come in.'

Starlight had to stoop to enter the shop. Lucy led them to the kitchen. Uncle Ben stood up when they entered and put down his French horn, which he had been polishing. He shook hands with Starlight, obviously pleased to see him.

'Where's your big bird?' Ben asked.

'He overwhelms some people, so I left him outside,' the captain replied.

'Well, he's very welcome here,' Lucy said.

Starlight opened a window and whistled. The next moment Benbow was standing on the ledge. He hopped inside and perched in the rafters overhead.

When they were seated around the table, Captain Starlight declined a cup of tea but accepted the offer of coffee, and then he told Lucy and Ben the purpose of his visit.

'I've come to ask your permission to take Abby and Spike on a trip, ma'am,' he said.

'Will they be gone long?' Aunt Lucy asked.

'Could be.'

'Will it be dangerous?'

'It might be, at that.'

'Why them?' Aunt Lucy said. 'They're so young.'

'Because they're special, ma'am. I think you already know that.'

Lucy nodded. 'Do they know about the Sea Witches?'

'We do now,' Abby replied.

'Why do you say they're *special*?' Ben asked.

Starlight turned to him. 'Benbow knew when he was three thousand miles away that Abby was in danger. He couldn't have had that premonition unless she possessed certain powers.'

'What are they?' asked Uncle Ben.

Starlight looked at him. 'To be honest, I don't yet know. But I'm sure she has them all the same.'

'What about Spike?'

'He speaks the language of the Seven Seas. Not many can do that.'

Lucy sat for a time looking at her niece, and then she said, 'You're going to look for my sister and her husband, aren't you?'

'We are, ma'am,' Starlight confirmed.

Lucy stood up. 'Then we can only wish you good luck.'

Despite Aunt Lucy's sadness, Abby felt happier than she could ever remember.

'When shall we go?' she asked.

'The sooner the better,' Starlight answered.

Lucy put a hand on Abby's shoulder. 'You're going to have something to eat before you go, young lady.'

It was growing dark when Captain Starlight finally steered the Atlantis Boat out of the secret cavern and into the open sea. He kept the speed low for the first few miles until they were well clear of the land. Spike and Abby sat in the snug little cabin drinking hot chocolate while Benbow perched dozing on a rail near the captain's elbow.

Abby had been surprised when Aunt Lucy and Uncle Ben hadn't objected to Starlight taking her and Spike off on such an adventure. She'd thought they would forbid them to go. Aunt Lucy clearly trusted Captain Starlight a great deal.

'Do you have radar?' Spike asked Starlight after a time.

The captain chuckled. 'Something much better than that, lad,' Starlight replied, and he passed his hand over the large crystal ball set in the control panel. Suddenly, through the windscreen, they could see the sea ahead as though it were as bright as day.

'Get ready,' Starlight said. 'I'm going to increase the speed now.' He pulled back on the throttle and the sleek little boat shot forward at an incredible pace. Although the sea was quite choppy, the craft stayed as steady and even as if it were crossing a boating lake in a park.

They saw other ships flash past in the darkness, fishing boats, cargo ships, a vast oil tanker and a ferryboat blazing with light. As they cut through the sea at a dazzling speed, Captain Starlight explained that the Atlantis Boat would not show up on the other ships' radar.

Finally, he altered course and said, 'We're entering the Thames Estuary now.' He eased back on the throttle and for a time they cruised on towards London where Abby and Spike could see the lights of the city glowing on the skyline.

'We stop here,' Captain Starlight said as they came to a halt beside a sleek sailing ship moored in an inlet of the river. The name *Ishmael* was painted on its prow.

'Climb aboard,' said Starlight, indicating a rope ladder hanging from the side. 'Welcome to my home.'

Spike looked over the side at the Atlantis Boat which was bobbing in the swell beside them. 'Aren't you going to tie her up, Captain?' he asked.

'No need for that, lad,' Starlight answered. He gave a short rising whistle and immediately, the Atlantis Boat sank below the surface of the river. 'She'll rest on the bottom until we need her again,' he added as he led them below through a hatchway.

The cabin was handsomely panelled in dark wood, trimmed with gleaming brass. Leather sofas cushioned the bulkheads. It was a little cold when they had taken off their Atlantis capes. Spike and Abby were surprised to find the cabin also served as an artist's studio. There was a large easel at one end, beneath a glass-covered hatch; and a table spread with paints. Brushes of all sizes stood in jars. There were paintings everywhere showing sailing ships through the ages.

'I'll light the stove to get some heat in here,' Starlight said, 'then we can make some hot drinks.' With that, he went above once more.

'What do you think he does with all these paintings?' Abby asked.

Before Spike could answer, Starlight had returned with a bundle of firewood and he answered her question. 'When I designed boats in Bright Town those were my plans,' he said.

'They don't look like boat builder's plans to me, Captain,' said Abby.

'Oh, we never bothered with those. I just used to do a painting. If the witches liked the look of it they would just spell it together.'

'I'd like to see that done,' Spike said.

'Perhaps you will one day, lad.'

As Starlight's coffee percolated, he fried some sausages and opened a large can of beans which he heated on the stove. They sat around a chart table and ate the supper.

'These beans are good,' Spike said.

'Boston baked beans, lad,' Starlight answered. 'Best in the world, even Benbow eats them.'

'Where is Benbow?' Abby asked. They hadn't seen him for some time.

'I've sent him off to look around,' Starlight said. 'He'll

be back before dawn.' He glanced at his watch. 'Time for you two to turn in. Your bunks are in the forward cabin.' He showed them the way to a little bathroom. 'Have a good wash, then put your capes back on. It might be a chilly night.'

Abby and Spike did as he suggested and quite soon they were lying on their bunks feeling sleepy. Abby could hear Starlight's footsteps on the deck above, then the sound of an accordion playing softly as she fell asleep.

The Lair of the Night Witches

Abby and Spike woke up in the faint light of a cold morning. Still snug in her Atlantis cape, Abby looked through the porthole above her bunk and saw the grey waters of the river dimpling with rain. Spike sat up in the bunk opposite and said, 'I can smell bacon and coffee.'

They got up and found Starlight in the galley making breakfast. 'It'll be ready in a minute,' he called out cheerfully. 'There's fresh bread in the stove.'

They enjoyed the breakfast. 'I really like your cooking, Captain Starlight,' Abby said looking down at her clean plate. 'My Aunt Lucy never fries anything.'

He smiled at the compliment. 'Well, I've had a long time to practise. It was at least a hundred and fifty years before I could make myself a good cup of coffee.'

'I've never made myself anything to eat,' said Spike. 'No, that's not quite true – I did peel a banana once.'

As he spoke, Benbow hopped through the hatchway.

'Did you find it?' Starlight asked.

The bird nodded.

When the breakfast things were cleared away, Starlight produced a large map and spread it on the chart table. 'This is where we're moored,' he said, pointing to the chart. 'Show us where they are, Benbow.'

Benbow tapped with his beak on the map and Starlight marked the spot.

'So that's the headquarters of the Night Witches,' Abby said. 'It's not very far.'

Starlight nodded. 'I thought they'd be around here someplace,' he said. 'Now, let's see how we're going to get in.' He produced an object shaped like a top from the pocket of his reefer jacket. 'This is another piece of equipment we found on the Atlantis Boat,' he explained. He placed it on the map where Benbow had pointed and set it spinning.

The top glowed with a bluish light as a hazy bubble appeared above it. The bubble grew, almost filling the entire cabin. Slowly, an image began to form within it — a bleak wasteland, ugly, wide and forbidding under a stormy, darkening sky.

In the centre was a great tangled pile of discarded rubbish. Rusting cars, old prams, battered washing machines, the skeletons of bicycles, discarded refrigerators, rotting boxes, squashed cardboard containers, rusty oil drums and battered tin cans. All stood on the edge of ragged marshland. Above it drifted old newspaper and plastic bags fluttering like liberated flags in the wind.

It all looked so bleak and sinister, Abby and Spike couldn't help shuddering. Captain Starlight said 'They've concealed their headquarters well.'

'What headquarters?' asked Spike.

The captain spoke to the spinning top. 'Show us the rest.'

The great heap of rubbish began to move as if a mighty beast were stirring beneath its surface. Then a dark yellow-ish fog formed above it all, obscuring the scene.

'Take the fog away,' Starlight instructed. Now they could see the hideous pile was reforming itself as some-thing began to emerge from the bowels of the earth. The tangle of objects started to assume the shape of a gigantic rough tower that rose higher and higher into the sky.

'Is this happening at this moment, Captain?' Abby asked.

Starlight studied some symbols on the skin of the bubble. 'No, this happened last evening. When the late shift of Night Witches came to do their work.'

No sooner had he spoken than the darkening sky about the tower of rubbish began to fill with a flock of black flut-tering figures that flitted through the sky like giant bats.

Gradually, it became clear that they were men and women wearing cloaks which were attached to their feet and hands. They circled the building before swooping down to cling to the outside. Then they crawled through cracks in the rubbish to gain entrance to the tower.

'I thought all witches rode broomsticks and looked silly,' Spike said quietly. 'This lot don't look at all funny.'

Captain Starlight shook his head. 'It's the cloaks that

enable Night Witches to fly. They can make themselves
seem smaller as well. When ordinary people see them,
they think they're just bats or birds.'

'What do you think they're doing now?' Abby asked.

'Show us the inside,' Starlight instructed softly.

The walls of rubbish became transparent and they could
see the witches scurrying about inside the tower. To Abby,
it seemed more like the hive of some giant insects. The
interior was formed to make passageways and corridors
that led to chambers of varying sizes. Some were so small
that only two or three witches used them; others were big
enough to contain hundreds. Abby could see there were
workshops, factory floors and laboratories.

At the centre there was a core of great steel girders that
housed banks of vast elevators. Massive steel cages, as large
as houses, groaned and hissed as they clanked between
floors. Some contained huge pieces of machinery in varying
stages of construction.

'Shark Boats,' Starlight said softly, pointing to the bubble. 'This is where they make them.' Then he moved his finger to another part of the building. Abby and Spike could see huge bubbling vats of oily black liquid. 'And this is where they make the stuff they mix with Ice Dust to make the Black Dust.'

'What are *they*?' asked Spike, pointing to strange creatures with powerful ape-like bodies that swarmed all over the machines. Sparks flew from their welding equipment and the noise of riveting hammers and metal grinders screeched and screamed like tortured animals.

The creatures wore tight black uniforms over their lumpy bodies, but their most disturbing aspects were their faces. Their coarse reddish hair was cropped close to their skulls so that the pink of their skin showed through. But their faces were hardly human at all. They had dog-like

snouts with canine tusks and small deep-set eyes that were blood red.

'Trolls,' Captain Starlight replied. 'Servants of the Night Witches.'

The machines they laboured over looked dangerous and forbidding to Abby. Night Witches flew above the trolls, hovering like insects to inspect their work. It did not look like a place inhabited by human beings at all.

'Why do some of the boats they're making look different?' Spike asked.

'They're all Shark Boats,' replied Starlight. 'But some of them are for cargo and some are submarines.'

'What do you think that one is?' asked Spike, pointing to yet another machine which was larger than any of the boats under construction. It looked like a great crouching insect.

'I'm not sure,' Starlight answered. 'But it looks as if it could fly.'

They watched as the trolls wheeled the machine into one of the massive elevators. It began to descend with its cargo. When the elevator reached ground level, they saw it unloaded into a mighty hall. One of the Night Witches climbed into the machine and gradually, like a giant insect flexing itself, the machine began to alter its shape. Wings emerged and what looked like beetle's legs thrust out from the body. It quivered for a moment and then stood still.

'Now I'm sure it's a flying machine,' Starlight said, as a group of Night Witches gathered on a raised dais before the massive device. Some sort of ceremony was about to take place. A throbbing sound of beating drums began and the massive hall began to fill with Night Witches. Some clung to the walls like bats as they waited.

Abby saw that another elevator was descending. It hissed to a halt and the gates opened. The Night Witches bowed low as a terrible figure emerged from the elevator.

It was a man, tall and powerful. He stood very straight and carried himself with an arrogant pride. His face was white as chalk and his features so gaunt there were deep hollows beneath his cheekbones. Under thin arched eyebrows, his nose was as sharply hooked as the beak of a bird of prey.

He looked as if he had no lips, just a slash of a mouth that curved down in a permanent scowl. A mane of matt-black hair hung down to his shoulders. There was no colour about his features except for his eyes. They were the same shape as a cat's and glowed like yellow fire in the dim light.

But it was his expression more than his appearance that chilled Abby. She could tell at a glance that there was no pity in the man, just pride and a dreadful cruelty. He was dressed in a strange costume of flowing black materials that floated around his body as though stirred by a night breeze, fleetingly taking the shape of demons, snakes and giant crawling insects.

'The Chief of the Night Witches,' Starlight whispered to Abby and Spike.

One of the bowing figures on the dais stood upright and addressed him. 'Great One, your new flying machine is ready for your inspection.'

The arrogant figure stepped forward and held up a hand. After a long pause he began. 'Night Witches, this is a memorable day in our history. The last part of my great plan is about to begin. The Light Witches are a spent force, their last stocks of Ice Dust are virtually exhausted. In Antarctica, our new mines are in full production. We have stockpiled our Black Ice weapons. Quite soon, we shall begin to exterminate the Light Witches.'

A great cheer welled up from the watching crowd. The Great One held up a hand and silence descended once again.

'When the Light Witches are destroyed, nothing shall stand between us and our final victory over the human race. A New World Order is about to begin and we shall be the masters. Soon I shall fly to Antarctica. From there, armed with our latest weapon, we shall launch our attack and the Light Witches will know an eternity of pain and suffering.'

Cheering filled the great hall until the Great One stepped forward and took a small glass bottle offered to him by one of the attendants. He walked to the flying machine and sprinkled black powder on to it. 'I name this machine *Darkness*. May the power of evil be with her whenever she flies,' he shouted. Then the throbbing drums and the cheering began again.

Once more, the Great One held up a hand. 'I am pleased with the work you have all done. You deserve a reward. As you know, we hold many captives at the mines. They are growing weak and their usefulness is almost over. We shall capture replacements.

'So I am going to declare a day of Night Witch sport. We shall bring all the captives we hold back here and you may each have one to destroy in the method that gives you the most amusement.'

The Witches began to howl with delight.

The spinning top began to wobble and the image in the bubble faded to nothing.

Abby Volunteers for a Dangerous Mission

Abby and Spike sat without speaking in the cabin of the *Ishmael* while Captain Starlight hunched at the chart table and thought about what they had seen in the bubble. Finally, he said, 'It doesn't look as if we have got much time. But we still need to know the exact location of the Ice Dust mine.'

Abby stood up. 'You say there must be a map inside their headquarters. I'll make myself invisible and go in and find it.'

Starlight nodded. 'It will be dangerous, Abby, but there's no other way.' He set the top spinning again and the image of the building reformed inside the bubble.

'Is there no way we can read the map just by looking in the bubble?' asked Spike, and Abby knew he was worried about her.

Starlight shook his head. 'We tried maximum magnification.

It just isn't close enough to read something as small as a map.'

Then he issued another command to the top. 'Show a weak spot in the Night Witch defences.' Immediately a tiny red light darted to a point on the roof of the fortress.

'Go as close as you can,' Starlight said, and the image enlarged. The red dot now hovered between the remains of an old bicycle and three rusty oil drums. They could all see what looked like the entrance to a narrow tunnel.

'How can Abby get up there?' Spike asked.

Starlight thought again, until Benbow hopped from where he had been dozing near a porthole and lay his head on Abby's shoulder. 'Well done, Benbow,' Starlight said. 'He'll fly you up there, Abby. But you'll have to practise making him invisible first.'

'How shall I start?' Abby replied.

'Begin with something small,' Starlight advised, and he placed a pebble in her hand.

Abby whistled her tune and vanished but the stone remained in view.

'Is there a trick to it?' she asked.

'I suppose so,' Starlight replied. 'But I can't help you with that. I've never been able to vanish myself so I don't know what it's like. You'll have to experiment for yourself.'

Determined to make it work, Abby whistled and whistled until Spike grew weary of seeing her vanish and reappear. 'I think I'll go for a swim,' he said eventually. 'That's the only way I'll manage to disappear.'

'Don't go too far from the boat,' Starlight said. 'We

might want you in a hurry.'

'I won't,' Spike said and he went up on deck. Abby's whistle came to him again as he dived from the deck rail.

Spike swam for ages, forgetting the time, until he became bored with the same stretch of river and returned to the *Ishmael*. When he climbed back on board, he called out, but there was no answer.

Hurrying below he found the cabin empty. Abby, Starlight and Benbow had all vanished. He was beginning to worry, when there was a laugh and he heard Abby whistle her tune in reverse. Suddenly, she, Captain Starlight and Benbow reappeared before him.

'I can do it, Spike. I can make other things invisible as well as myself,' she called out happily.

Spike was relieved, but tried not to show it. 'So there'll be no end to the tricks you'll play on me now,' he replied drily.

'Cheer up, lad,' Starlight said. 'We've got Boston baked beans again for tea.'

'Oh, good,' Spike said, his humour immediately restored.

'When shall I go?' Abby asked when the meal was finished. Starlight looked out of the hatchway. A steady rain was beating down and more heavy clouds were rolling in from the west.

'It'll be dark soon, I don't think there's enough light left. Best go in just after dawn. Night Witches like to work in darkness. They're at their slowest early in the morning.'

'I'll be ready,' Abby said, feeling a sudden lurch of fear as she remembered the promise she'd heard the chief of the Night Witches make about their captives.

Flight into Danger

The following morning, the rain clouds had passed away and dawn was colouring the sky with pale pink clouds when Captain Starlight woke Abby and Spike.

'I always start with a good breakfast,' he said, serving them plates of bacon and eggs.

When they'd finished, Starlight looked at his watch. 'The Night Witch late shift will be leaving now. Time to go, Abby,' he said. 'Just one more thing. I think I've still got a pinch of Ice Dust somewhere.' He hunted through a sea chest and produced a flask.

'Hmm, this should be enough,' he said thoughtfully. 'Stand still, lad.'

'Why?' said Spike?

'I've never seen anyone as pale as you, Spike. Maybe it's caused by witchcraft.'

'But I don't want to change,' Spike protested as Starlight shook the contents over him.

They waited in anticipation for a few moments. But nothing happened. Starlight seemed surprised. 'That's strange, it must be the real you,' he said, perplexed. 'Well, I've sailed the Seven Seas many times over but I've never seen anyone quite like you, lad. Do you mind being so different?'

'Well, it hasn't caused me any problems so far. If I can get on with a tiger shark, I can get on with anybody.'

'Do you really know a tiger shark, Spike?' Abby was impressed. She thought she knew everything about him by now. 'You never told me.'

'I didn't want you to worry. He's not a bad chap, actually. Mind you, I've only met him *after* he's had his lunch.'

They went on deck. Starlight whistled for the Atlantis Boat and it resurfaced from the river-bed. 'All aboard,' he said and they set off up river. After a time, Starlight stopped the engine. 'Over there,' he said, pointing into the marshes. 'That's the Night Witch headquarters.'

They looked over a wide expanse of mud flats to where the tower of rubbish stood partially shrouded by a yellow-ish mist. While Abby and Spike watched, Starlight attached two straps to Benbow's feet. 'Just put your hands through these loops,' he explained, 'and you'll be safe until you want to let go.'

Abby did as Starlight instructed.

'All set?' he asked.

'Yes, Captain,' Abby replied. She took a deep breath and looked up at the pale blue sky above her.

'Have you got the seashell I gave you handy?'

Abby patted her pocket. 'Got it.'

'Now whistle your tune,' said Starlight. 'And when you take hold of Benbow's feet he'll become invisible as well.'

Abby did as he instructed and Benbow rose into the air and paused, wings flapping, above her head. Abby reached up and put her hands into the leather loops. She looked up and saw the great bird vanish.

There was a sudden jerk and, moments later, she found herself soaring into the sky with the river Thames looking smaller and smaller beneath her. As Benbow flew higher she could see the whole expanse of the estuary and the sea beyond.

Far below her, she could still see the Atlantis Boat, although Spike and Captain Starlight were too small for her to make out. Benbow flew in a wide circle and she could feel the rush of air on her face. Then she saw they were about to land on top of the Night Witches' headquarters.

The Court of the Night Witches

*J*ust before Abby slipped her hands from the straps she spoke to Benbow. 'Keep circling the building. If I need you in a hurry I'll shout out,' she whispered.

Benbow nodded and took off again.

Abby crouched down in sudden fear because she could see a few of the strange, ape-like figures prowling among the tangled rubbish. Then she remembered she was invisible and slowly stood up.

She whispered into her seashell to tell Starlight about the trolls nearby.

'Take care,' he said. 'They can be very dangerous.'

'What exactly are trolls, Captain Starlight?' she asked softly.

'A very nasty type of creature that used to be found in the forests of central Europe,' he answered. 'We never had them in America. They used to steal children, so they say.'

'What for?'

Starlight paused. 'Well, the story said they liked to keep

them as slaves until the children grew big enough to eat. Night Witches like trolls because they're stupid and wicked but easy to train. Best to keep clear of them, Abby.'

'I'll keep as clear as I can,' she replied, looking up. Benbow was visible now and still hovering above her. Two of the prowling trolls nearby stared at him, momentarily puzzled by his sudden appearance. Abby shuddered to see their snouty faces gazing into the sky, as if they were sniffing for food.

She quickly found the entrance to the tunnel and reeled back for a moment, gasping at the dreadful smell. It was like a mixture of bad eggs, sewers and old boiled cabbage water. Abby knew roughly where she was heading. When they had studied the inside of the building earlier, she had noticed a room where the walls were covered in maps. It was off to one side of a much larger chamber that was filled with rows of empty benches.

Now, she hurried through the tunnel. It curved down through the building in a steep slope. She was glad to see there were signposts and notices. Occasionally, Night Witches swooped above her and she had to keep ducking her head.

Suddenly, ahead, she saw a flurry of witches gathering to enter a room. The sign above the door said *Court Number One* in bold letters and below, in smaller type, *Leading to Trophy Room* — exactly what she'd been seeking.

Although they disgusted her, Abby joined the throng to squeeze inside the chamber. She slipped into a space behind the door. Night Witches were taking the seats on the banks of benches that lined each side of the room. Abby could now see that it was furnished as a courtroom with a dock for a prisoner and a raised bench for a judge.

Like the rest of the building, the room smelt awful and the Night Witches were all scratching themselves as they gabbled together in subdued voices. Most of them had ragged yellowish teeth and Abby noticed that even the younger ones often showed black gaps.

Now, Abby could study them in detail. They were an ugly bunch, some fat and some thin, and all ages. But, apart from the black cloaks they wore, the only thing they had in common was how grubby they were. She had never seen so much greasy hair and ingrained dirt and so many dirty fingernails.

The older men wore stained suits and the younger ones dirty casual clothes. The women all seemed to favour tatty, dull-coloured dresses that trailed along the floor. Judging from their fish-white complexions they obviously didn't spend much time in daylight.

When the court was full, a witch who was standing at a table below the judge's bench banged on the table with a gavel and said, 'Silence. All rise for her supreme eminence, Judge Stakeheart.'

The Night Witches rose to their feet and a very old woman with a face covered in warts and straggly hair entered. She was wearing a cloak, tattered and green with age. It flapped around her as she shuffled towards the high seat behind the bench.

'Be seated,' the clerk commanded. 'Bring in the prisoner.'

A door opened at the back of the court and two trolls entered escorting a young woman who hung her head so that long greasy hair obscured her face. She was enveloped in a grubby Night Witch's cloak.

'Remove her cloak,' the judge ordered.

One of the trolls wrenched it off to reveal that the prisoner was wearing a clean, pale yellow dress. The other troll snatched the greasy wig from her head, and shining red hair tumbled about her shoulders.

There was a collective gasp of surprise from the court. The young woman threw back her head and gazed around the court defiantly.

'What are the charges?' Judge Stakeheart asked.

An extremely fat Night Witch, who had been lolling at one of the tables in front of the bench and scratching the stains on his waistcoat, rose to his feet and said, 'If it please Your Eminence, this creature known to us, until she was apprehended, as Gretchen Cringe, is in fact a Light Witch! She joined our order under false pretences to gain access to our secrets.'

'What evidence do you have?'

'The evidence of your own eyes, Your Eminence. As you observe, beneath her cloak she wears clean clothes. When she was examined, there were no lice or fleas about her person, and...' the accuser hesitated.

'It is so horrible, Your Eminence, I do not want to offend your sensibilities.'

'Thank you for your delicacy, but pray continue.'

'She smells of flowers.'

This revelation caused a moan of horror to ripple through the court.

'How was she apprehended?' the judge asked when the court was silent.

'She was trying to release a polar bear that was the subject of experiments in the research department.'

'Enough,' the judge commanded. She addressed the accused.

'Do you have anything to say before I pass sentence?'

The girl in the dock looked around the room with contempt. 'Only that I am Sally Oak of the Ancient Order of Light Witches. I am immune to your punishments, as you well know. I demand to be released immediately.'

The judge gave a sharp laugh. 'You are quite wrong, young woman. It was once the case that Light Witches were immune to our spells, but our strength has increased mightily since then. We have devised a machine, powered by Black Dust that will soon be used on all your brethren. Therefore, I sentence you to be atomized and to spend all eternity in the prison we have devised for Light Witches.'

The court started to applaud but Judge Stakeheart held up a claw-like hand. 'Bring in the prototype of the Atomizer.'

A door opened and a group of trolls pushed in a machine that looked to Abby like a huge flashlight mounted on wheels. Thick cables spewed from the end.

'So you can fully appreciate the severity of your

punishment, Sally Oak,' the judge continued, 'we shall demonstrate the Atomizer on the polar bear you tried to release. Bring it in.'

More trolls entered with a great white bear that was secured with chains. The trolls were armed with batons that gave electric shocks to the creature. They positioned it before the Atomizer.

'Begin,' the judge ordered, and one of the trolls pulled a lever at the side of the machine. There was a sound like the distant crying of a lost child and, to Abby's horror, a clear rectangle formed around the bear and began to shrink until it was smaller than a matchbox. The Night Witches sent up shrieks of approval

'Hand it to the prisoner,' Judge Stakeheart ordered.

Sally Oak took the tiny object from the troll and held it tenderly. 'Poor bear,' she said and tears trickled down her cheeks. When she looked up, her eyes were blazing defiantly. 'A curse on you Night Witches for your vile cruelties. What has this poor creature done to you that you should torture it so?'

'Save your pity for yourself,' the judge answered, and turned to the trolls. 'Carry out the sentence.'

They did as they were ordered and the process was repeated on Sally Oak. When she was reduced to the size of the bear, a troll handed both cubes to the judge who studied them for a moment, cackling, then placed them on the bench in front of her. 'They can stay here for all eternity,' she said, and shuffled from the court. When she had departed, the rest of the Night Witches scrambled out, pushing and shoving one another as they left the room.

Abby waited until the room was quite clear before tip-toeing across the creaking floor. She took the two cubes the judge had left on the bench and placed them carefully in her pocket before entering a smaller chamber with the sign *Trophy Room* over the door.

The walls were covered with documents and above each was a demon's head carved in wood.

Abby studied the captions beneath the documents. Most told of spells and curses or of the dreadful things the Night Witches had done to people in the past. Others were accounts of trials conducted in the courtroom next door.

Finally, she came to one that was slightly different to the others. It was made of some kind of darker parchment covered with tiny inscriptions, and was pinned to the wall with two small daggers. The caption read: 'The Story and Maps of Mordoc's Land.'

This must be it, she thought, and was surprised that there were no guards in the room. She glanced about her before pulling out the daggers that held the scroll.

Immediately, the blank eyes of the carved demon's head above it glowed with life.

'Thief, thief, the curse of Mordoc on you,' the demon's head boomed out. Abby looked at the head in sudden horror and glanced around her in fear. She didn't notice there was another scroll of parchment behind the one she had taken. It had fallen to the floor.

Quickly, she rolled up the first document and tucked it inside her Atlantis cape, then she ran from the room. For a moment, she leaned against the wall of the corridor, her heart beating so fast she thought the sound would surely alert a group of Night Witches who were still lingering outside the courtroom. But they only looked about them in confusion at the sound of the booming from the demon's head.

One of them called out. 'There must be a thief in the building. Sound the alarm!'

'I can smell them,' one of the other witches called out.

'So can I,' shouted another. 'The smell is sweet — it's a little girl. Set the trolls after her.'

Abby started to run. There was another noise up ahead — the slamming of doors in the tunnel she had used to enter. She ducked into another room. It had no furniture but was filled with Night Witches who were watching an instructor draw symbols on the filthy floor.

The instructor was saying, 'This is what you mark on a house if you want the premises infested with cockroaches—' she broke off to shriek, 'I smell an intruder!'

Another witch began to sniff the foul air. 'Little girl, it smells of little girl!'

'An invisible girl!' one of them shrieked. 'Quick, form a circle.'

One of the witches slammed the door shut and all of them lined up around the walls holding hands.

As they began to close in on her, Abby could see that she would have to act quickly.

Looking around in desperation, she saw there was one small window glazed with black glass. She darted through a narrowing gap beneath the clasped hands of the encircling Night Witches and pulled on the window handle. The frame was clogged with old deposits of sooty grease.

Abby gave it a good wrench. It flew open and daylight flooded into the room. The Night Witches cringed back in horror. 'Ahgggh! Fresh air, fresh air!' they shrieked.

Abby paused on the windowsill and saw that she was still high above the ground. Below her, the Atlantis Boat at the river's edge looked like a toy. Behind her, the Night Witches were shielding their faces from the light with their cloaks, but still their hands were scrabbling for her.

She hesitated only a moment, then whistled the tune that made her visible.

As filthy hands clawed for her, she shouted out, 'Benbow, here I come...' and she leaped into the void. Abby tumbled over twice and all the contents of her pocket fell out. She just managed to catch the two cubes but the seashell plummeted out of reach.

She could feel the air rushing past her as she hurtled towards the ground but she remembered to keep her hands out. Suddenly, she felt herself seized in a powerful grip. Benbow had swooped down and now held her safely in his grasp.

Within moments, they landed on the deck of the Atlantis Boat.

'Quick get below,' Starlight instructed.

Abby glanced up and saw a great flock of Night Witches hurtling down on them like a storm of whirling bats.

As she raced below, she could see they were almost upon the boat before it sank beneath the waters of the river.

'I'm taking her out into the middle of the channel — *fast!*' Starlight shouted. 'Strap yourselves in tight.'

As Spike and Abby fastened their safety belts, the little boat surged forward with such speed they felt themselves forced against the back of their seats.

When Starlight judged they were well clear of any pursuing Night Witches, he throttled back and allowed the Atlantis Boat to sink to the bed of the river, where it came to rest.

Only Benbow seemed unaffected by Abby's narrow escape. He settled down in one of the seats and seemed to doze off. Spike let out a long sigh, as if he had been holding his breath for a some time.

'Well done, Abby! Now, show me what you've got,' Starlight said.

She reached inside her cape and produced the parchment and the two tiny cubes.

'What are these?' Starlight asked, holding up the cubes.

Abby explained about the Atomizer. When she had finished, Starlight found a notebook and a large magnifying glass. First he looked at Sally Oak in the glass, then he wrote in very small letters on the notebook:

CAN YOU READ THIS?

He held the magnifying glass to Sally Oak's cube again and saw that the tiny figure was nodding.

He then wrote:

WE WILL KEEP YOU SAFE UNTIL THE LIGHT WITCHES FIND A SOLUTION TO YOUR PLIGHT.

Sally Oak nodded again. Then she held up her hands and began to move them rapidly.

'Sign language,' Starlight explained.

'Do you understand it?' Abby asked.

'You understand a lot of things when you're as old as I am,' Starlight answered. 'She says *thank you*.'

He made signs to show he understood her and that she would be safe in Abby's pocket. Then he turned to Abby again and said. 'What about the map?'

Starlight unrolled the document Abby handed to him. 'This is bad,' he said.

'Why?' Abby asked, craning to look over his shoulder. The parchment was quite blank.

'But it had a map on it when I took it from the wall,' she said.

'Did anything else happen?' Starlight asked.

Abby thought for a moment. 'There was a demon head above it,' she said.

'Go on,' Starlight urged.

'I thought it was carved from wood but it spoke.'

'What did it say? Try to remember the exact words.'

Abby paused. 'I'm pretty sure it said, "Thief, thief, the Curse of Mordoc on you".'

Starlight sat down and crossed his arms. 'The Curse of Mordoc... the Curse of Mordoc,' he repeated. Then he shook his head and sighed deeply before he lay the blank scroll on the chart table. 'There's nothing for it, we'll just have to consult the Master of the Light Witches.'

'You don't seem very keen,' Abby said.

Starlight shook his head. 'I'm not,' he replied. 'Sea Witches are fine, salt of the earth, but the English Light Witches are a different kettle of fish all together.'

'How do you mean?' asked Spike. 'I thought the idea was that they were supposed to be good.'

'Oh, they're not bad,' Starlight said quickly. 'It's just... well, they can be a bit difficult. There's always a lot of temperament with English Light Witches.'

'So they're different to American Light Witches?' Spike said.

'Quite different,' Starlight answered. 'American Light Witches tend to be plain folk. Mostly from the country, you see.'

'So why are English Light Witches different?'

Starlight scratched his head before he answered. 'Much of what they do is a bit flashy — conjuring, acting and the like. I suppose it gives them airs and graces.'

'What is the Master of the English Light Witches like?' Abby asked. 'Is he difficult to deal with?'

Starlight shook his head again. 'I've said enough. You'll have to make up your own minds. Maybe I'm a bit prejudiced. I've always been too much of a plain man to get on too well with English Light Witches.'

Starlight looked at his watch. 'I think I know where I can find him this evening.' He looked up at the sky. 'It's a fine day. Let's do some fishing until it's time to go.'

Starlight found some rods and the three of them sat on the little deck of the Atlantis Boat hooking herrings, which they fed to Benbow, until the setting sun cast long shadows on the water. Then Starlight switched on the engine. 'I suppose we'd better get under way,' he said.

'Where are we going,' Spike asked. 'Is it far?'

Starlight increased the throttle on the engine a little before he answered. 'The Alhambra Theatre, Shaftesbury Avenue, London W1.'

The Man Who Would Not be King

When twilight came, Starlight set off up the river Thames with the evening tide. As they approached London, the lights of the city sparkled and danced in the choppy waters of the river as if they were afloat on a carpet of jewels.

'Now, this is what I call an adventure,' said Abby.

'It certainly is,' agreed Spike. 'The most exciting thing that ever happens in Speller is when Mrs Porter's goat gets loose in the town square.'

'Do they have goats here, Captain Starlight?' Abby asked.

'Not that I know of,' replied the captain with a smile.

'No goats!' said Spike, disappointed. 'Perhaps London's more boring than I thought it would be.'

Captain Starlight finally brought the Atlantis Boat to a halt at a landing stage. A big pleasure boat was just casting off, its band playing dance music. Abby thought of Uncle Ben and felt a pang of homesickness

'Embankment pier,' Starlight announced. 'This is as

good a place as any to moor.'

They disembarked and waited quietly while a few strag-
glers from the last boat to dock made their way up the
steps. When the coast was clear, Starlight whistled the boat
to rest on the river bed.

When they had passed from the pier to the pavement
the world seemed suddenly filled with hurrying crowds and
pounding traffic. Buses, lorries and motor cars thundered
along the wide road that ran beside the river. Captain
Starlight took their hands and strode off towards Shaftesbury Avenue.

At first, Abby and Spike were almost overwhelmed by
the bustling crowds and the roar of traffic that boomed at
them from all sides. Aunt Lucy had told them a great deal
about the history of the city, so they made Starlight stop in
Trafalgar Square to take a good look at Nelson's Column.

Benbow perched on one of the bronze lions at the base,
but soon flew away when a crowd gathered to feed him
with the bird-seed they'd bought for the pigeons.

The lights from the shop windows were dazzlingly inviting, but the crowds of strangers and noisy traffic still made
them feel a little bit nervous. Starlight held their hands
tightly as they hurried along the pavements, keeping up
with his long strides.

'I think I may prefer Mrs Porter's goat escaping to all
these crowds,' Abby said to Spike.

He nodded. 'Perhaps you can have too much excitement.'

'I'm pretty sure this is Shaftesbury Avenue,' Starlight

announced finally, as he stopped for a few moments outside a fire station. 'If my memory serves me still, the Alhambra Theatre is further down here on the right. Come on.'

They passed several theatres ablaze with lights, where people were queueing to buy tickets for the evening performance, but Starlight finally stopped before a darkened building that was boarded up and looked abandoned. The posters on the billboards were faded and torn and the windows in the doors were coated with grime.

'Dear me,' Starlight said softly. 'The Light Witches really have seen better days.'

'Why are we stopping here, Captain?' Abby asked.

'The Master of the Light Witches is Sir Chadwick Street, actor, manager and owner of this theatre. It's also the headquarters of the Light Witches — but the general public don't know that.'

'How do we get in?' Abby asked.

Starlight put his shoulder to one of the doors and heaved. After a moment it began to open, slowly. As a narrow crack appeared, three fat brown rats scurried out and set off, dodging through the traffic to cross the road.

'I thought rats only deserted sinking ships,' Spike said.

With one more mighty heave, Starlight managed to widen the gap enough for them to squeeze through. They stood for a moment in the dark stillness, breathing the stale air. The captain had a small bottle of St Elmo's fire. By its dim light, they crossed the great gloomy lobby and entered the doors that led to the stalls. A voice was booming rather sadly across the empty rows of seats.

'I think perhaps you'd better make us invisible, Abby,' Starlight whispered. 'I'm not sure what kind of a reception I can expect. Whistle your tune softly and we'll all hold hands.'

Abby did so and when they had vanished they tiptoed into the stalls and sat down in the front row. The voice they had heard earlier was now echoing around them.

'Now is the winter of our discontent...' There was a long pause before the voice continued. 'What truth there is in those words penned by the immortal Bard of Avon.' The figure that spoke stood at the front of the stage, close to the orchestra pit, facing the stalls. Two dim paraffin lamps lit the scene. Behind him was a long table where a dejected group of people were seated. 'That's Sir Chadwick Street, Master of the Light Witches,' Captain Starlight whispered to Abby and Spike.

Abby studied the man. He was wearing a battered, wide-brimmed tweed hat together with a voluminous green cape carelessly thrown over his shoulders. Beneath the cape he wore a boldly checked three-piece suit, careful-ly cut to show his long wiry frame to its best advantage.

His elegant boots were as tight as dancing pumps but the leather was cracked and patched. Although the overall effect was rather grand, his clothes had obviously seen bet-ter days. His flowing scarlet bow-tie was limp and the high collar of his shirt was frayed, as were the cuffs of his suit.

For a moment he stood quite still, then with a theatrical

flourish he swung his head round to present his profile. Marmalade-coloured side-whiskers framed his face and covered the length of his lantern jaw. His complexion was pale and a large Roman nose rose from dramatically hollow cheeks. His bright blue eyes were hooded and his full mouth smiled sadly, but his heavy jaw jutted forward in defiance.

Suddenly, he darted across the stage with an extraordinary lopsided gait. Although his legs were obviously of the same length he limped heavily and held one shoulder forward as though there were something heaped on his back. Then he snarled, *'Methinks a dreadful gloom has loured upon our house. The very air we breathe offends my nostrils.'* His voice boomed around the theatre and each word was perfectly clear.

Abby flinched nervously. Had he, like the Night Witches, caught scent of her?

One of the people seated at the table looked up. She was pretty and younger than the rest, with pale hair piled on top of her head and a pair of spectacles, mended with tape, perched on the end of her tilted nose.

'S-sorry, Master,' she said hesitantly. 'They haven't had an opportunity to air the theatre since our last meeting. Shall I get them to open the stage door?'

'No, have them leave it as it is,' he replied with a weary wave. 'We might as well breathe the air that so matches our foul condition.'

'As you wish, Master,' the young woman replied quickly.

'Are the brethren of our council all assembled?' he asked.

'The call has gone out, Master,' replied a fat man with a completely bald head and a large drooping moustache. 'We're just waiting for the Grand Treasurer. He should be here any minute.'

The Master slumped into a shabby but ornate chair that creaked alarmingly under his weight. Drawing himself forward he commanded, 'Then send in Hissquick the Sorcerer.'

Abby leaned closer to the invisible Starlight and whispered, 'Are sorcerers different to Light Witches?'

'Yes,' he answered softly. 'Sorcerers broke away from witches hundreds of years ago.'

'What do they do?'

'You'll see in a minute,' Starlight whispered.

Abby nodded and looked about her in the gloom. High above them she saw Benbow perched on a chandelier. He appeared to be asleep. 'He doesn't seem very impressed,' thought Abby.

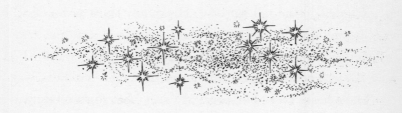

The Sorry State of the Light Witches

S ir Chadwick's call for the sorcerer was still echoing around the auditorium when an extraordinary man with a long wand under his arm strolled on to the stage. He was carrying a black box, which he placed at the Master's feet.

The new arrival was enormously fat with a long ginger beard reaching down to his waist. The purple cloak and the high conical hat perched upon his head glittered with thousands of tiny lights.

Sir Chadwick leaned back and looked with displeasure at the figure in the tall hat. 'So, Hissquick, what news of a cure for my dreadful affliction?' he snapped.

The fat man gestured towards the box with his wand. 'I have something new to try, Master of the Light Witches.'

'Make haste then, Sorcerer. My very bones grow weary of the irksome part I play.'

The Sorcerer held up his hands and began to speak in a sing-song voice. 'I have consulted my colleagues at the Royal

Society of Warlocks, Sorcerers and Ancient Apothecaries. They have recommended this treatment but they wish me to state unequivocally that there is no guarantee of success.'

'Yes, yes, man,' Sir Chadwick replied wearily. 'I know the knavish tricks of all you cursed fellows. "No guarantee of success" are words with which you insure all your failures. What foolish king did warrant you to steal from toiling Light Witches?'

'We received our royal crest from Aelfric the Bad, in the sixth century,' the Sorcerer replied stiffly. 'And let me remind you with all due respect, that you brought this problem upon yourself.'

Sir Chadwick leaned forward with an angry expression. 'Guard your tongue, Sorcerer. I am leader of the Light Witches and still outrank you in the Grand Order of Magic.'

The fat sorcerer stared back fearlessly. 'And let me remind you, Master of the Light Witches, that when you first came to me, pleading for help, you found it impossible to remember the part of Richard III.'

Sir Chadwick leaned even further forward in his seat and spoke in an ominously low voice. 'And now I can play no other. Remember, it is I who led the crusade against the Night Witches. And you rely on me for protection. But now, I cannot cease to play the role of Shakespeare's villain, Richard. You have made me a laughing stock.'

The sorcerer waved airily. 'There are side effects to all our spells. It's a small price to pay for all you've gained.'

'Gained! Gained?' Sir Chadwick roared. 'I have *gained*

nothing but the reputation of a clown.'

Once more the sorcerer raised his hand to calm Sir Chadwick. With a sweeping gesture towards the box at his feet, he added. 'As I said earlier, I have prepared another potion.' He opened the box, took out a glass bottle and handed it to Sir Chadwick. 'Drink this,' he instructed.

Abby leaned towards Captain Starlight and whispered. 'Does he really think he's winning the battle against the Night Witches?'

The captain nodded. 'That's been the trouble with Light Witches all along. They tend to be terrible optimists.'

Without hesitation, the Master drank the potion.

'Aggggh!' he cried, clutching his throat and staggering about the stage moaning loudly.

'Now he's playing, Dr Jekyll,' the Sorcerer said in a stage whisper to the startled Light Witches sitting at the table. 'He really is a terrible old ham.'

After a moment, Sir Chadwick stood up straight and tried a few paces across the stage. He did it without limping.

'I'm cured!' he called out triumphantly. 'Cured at last.'

'Well, that's that,' the sorcerer said, hurriedly moving towards the door. 'Glad to be of assistance. I'll send my bill as usual. Just remember, there may be the odd side effect to this potion as well.' Then he was gone.

At the sorcerer's exit another figure hurried on to the stage — a red-faced man in a scruffy overcoat and cloth cap. He wheeled in a coffin-shaped metal contraption. The scent of fried onions wafted across the stalls.

'Sorry to be late, Master,' he called out. I had a sudden rush of business in Piccadilly Circus.'

The Master pressed a hand to his forehead. 'Has it come to this? The Grand Treasurer of the Illustrious Order of Light Witches — selling hot dogs to tourists.'

'Would you care for one, Master?'

Sir Chadwick gave a slight wave of his hand. 'Not too much mustard.'

Following his lead, the other Light Witches gathered around the treasurer to give their orders.

When they were finally reseated, Sir Chadwick rapped on the table and said, 'I now bring this meeting to order. Steward, are all present and accounted for?'

A man so thin his tattered clothes flapped about his spindly body, leaned forward and said, 'All present now, Master.'

Sir Chadwick nodded. 'Minutes of the last meeting.'

The steward cleared his voice. 'It was agreed we'd go on doing exactly what you wanted done, Master.'

'Excellent. First item on the agenda: financial report.'

The treasurer stood up and said, 'Our finances are much the same, Master.' He reached into the pocket of his overcoat and placed a few bank notes and two handfuls of loose change on the table. 'At this precise moment we have about seven pounds and twenty-eight pence in our possession.'

The Master leaned forward. 'And how do you think the Night Witches are doing?'

'We estimate they had a good three months, Master.'

'How good?'

'I understand they made more than two billion pounds.'

'And how did they do that?'

'Their new anti-hay-fever pills.'

Sir Chadwick was puzzled for a moment. 'How can they be manufacturing an anti-hay-fever pill? It's not like the Night Witches to make something that actually makes people feel better.'

The treasurer shook his head. 'They gave the people hay fever in the first place. The pills cure the hay fever but give you a bad headache and dreadfully smelly feet.'

'I see,' exclaimed Sir Chadwick. 'Ingenious. And I suppose they're now working on something that cures the headache and smelly feet and gives you something else even worse.'

'Undoubtedly, Master,' the treasurer replied.

'Any other business?' Sir Chadwick said sighing.

The young woman with pale hair got to her feet and timorously held up a hand. She was clad in a fairly smart but ill-fitting business suit and the tail of her white shirt was hanging outside the waistband of her skirt.

'Remind me who you are and what you do again?' Sir Chadwick asked casually. He seemed to be losing interest in the proceedings.

'It's me, Hilda Bluebell, Master. As well as being an actress in the company, I've just been made Director of Research and Development. You also made me your personal assistant.'

'Oh, yes, Hilda, I didn't recognize you in your latest outfit.'

'You said you wanted me to keep a watch on any new developments the Night Witches came up with.'

'Of course. So, have they got anything we don't know about?'

'Yes, Master. I heard from our spy, Sally Oak, that they've been developing a new type of acid rain. We think they've perfected it.'

Sir Chadwick sniffed. 'There's nothing new about acid rain. They developed that years ago.'

Hilda Bluebell coughed. 'This type of acid rain really is new, Master. It falls indoors.'

Sir Chadwick sat up. 'Indoors! They can make acid rain fall *inside* houses now?'

'Yes, Master.'

'Do you know how they do it?'

'Yes.'

'Demonstrate it.'

'In here, Master?'

'Of course. It would be pointless to demonstrate it outside, wouldn't it?'

Hilda Bluebell got up and rummaged in her copious handbag. Eventually she produced a small box of powder, took a handful, and began to prance about the room, sprinkling it and chanting as she danced.

'Black rain fall,
and cover all.
Matters not to where you flee,
something terrible you'll see.
Nature now is out of kilter,
houses cannot give you shelter.'

As she recited, Sir Chadwick turned to the treasurer. 'Do they still use these techniques, reciting verse and so on? I thought the Night Witches prided themselves on being modern?'

As he spoke, a soft black rain began to fall inside the theatre, and to Abby's consternation, a dim outline of the three of them began to take shape.

'Can't you make the rain disappear as it falls on us, Abby?' Captain Starlight hissed.

'I'm trying to,' she said. 'But something seems to be blocking my powers.'

'Black Dust!' Starlight muttered. 'It must contain Black Dust. This could mean trouble.'

What Captain Starlight owes the Light Witches

Hilda Bluebell was the first to notice the shadowy forms appearing in the stalls. 'Look, look!' she warned. 'I can see some invisible people.'

Without turning his head, Sir Chadwick sighed in weary irritation. 'How can you *see* something that is invisible?' he asked. 'I really do expect precision from somebody in your position of responsibility.'

'But look, Master,' she continued. 'It's the acid rain.'

Sir Chadwick followed the direction of her pointing finger and let out a sudden shout. 'Intruders! Close all the exits. Bar the doors.' He peered down at the shadowy forms of Spike, Abby and Captain Starlight sitting in the stalls.

'Does anyone remember a spell that will reveal them totally?'

'I could give it a try, Master,' Hilda Bluebell offered, suddenly more confident.

'Well, you'd better get on with it, my dear,' he urged.

Hilda looked thoughtful for a few moments and then began to recite:

> *'Vase of flowers, bowl of fruit,*
> *let this spell be one to suit*
> *all occasions we may fear*
> *And make these people reappear.'*

'Excellent,' said Sir Chadwick. 'I couldn't have done it better myself.'

'Thank you, Master,' said Hilda, blushing rather prettily.

Now Abby could see they were slowly becoming even more visible.

'Who are you? And how dare you enter these premises uninvited?' said Sir Chadwick, blinking in their direction. Then he looked up in irritation. 'Someone stop that blasted rain.'

Sir Chadwick pointed an accusing finger at Starlight and the two children. 'What are you doing here spying on us?' he demanded.

'Don't you know it's rude to point?' Abby replied, determined not to be frightened.

'Keep a civil tongue in your head,' the Master snapped. 'Or I'll turn you all into frogs.'

'How will we be able to answer your questions if we're frogs?' Abby continued defiantly.

'Silence!' bellowed Sir Chadwick, and turned to Hilda

Bluebell. 'They're Night Witch spies. Conjure me up a giant rat and a cage so we can put them all in it together.'

'May I have a minute before I attempt that, Master?' Hilda Bluebell answered. 'I'm having a little difficulty turning off the rain.'

'Can't you just send it somewhere else?'

'I can try,' Hilda replied.

'Please make it quick,' Sir Chadwick pleaded. 'It's ruining my last good suit.'

'Where would you like it to go?' Hilda asked nervously.

The Master turned to her. 'I really don't care, just as long as it's not falling on me.' He turned to the other Light Witches huddled around the table, their collars now turned up against the downpour. 'If none of you can help, at least offer the girl some encouragement.'

Now they began to call out, 'Go on Hilda…' 'Well done, Hilda…' 'You can do it, girl.'

Sir Chadwick gave them a glance full of withering scorn, then Hilda held up her hands and began to chant:

> 'Let this acid rain depart
> and break someone else's heart.
> Find a nasty Night Witch nest
> and dirty rain will do the rest.'

Suddenly, there was a great whooshing sound and the rain was drawn out of the theatre. Sir Chadwick held up one of the dim lamps and inspected the three intruders. When he came to Captain Starlight, he hesitated. 'Don't I know you?' he asked.

Captain Starlight gave a slight bow. 'You do, Sir. Captain Adam Starlight of Massachusetts. Sometime chief designer of ships for the Sea Witches of Bright Town. May I present my companions, Abby Clover and Spike, townsfolk of Speller.'

Sir Chadwick stroked his chin. 'Adam Starlight, of course. I met you long ago in Bright Town in happier days. You were also known as the Ancient Mariner, I think.'

Starlight bowed again.

'We've been waiting a long time to catch up with you, Captain Starlight.' Sir Chadwick said softly. 'What happened to the Ice Dust you took from Bright Town? You were supposed to deliver it to us.'

'It's a long story,' Starlight replied.

Sir Chadwick nodded. 'Then you'd better come up here and tell me all about it.'

The trio trooped up on to the stage. Sir Chadwick sat down on his creaking throne and gestured towards the captain. 'Now, tell us, Captain Starlight, what happened to that casket of Ice Dust? We had a message from the last defenders of Bright Town that you would bring it here.'

'I had other uses for it,' Starlight replied.

Sir Chadwick leaned forward. 'Let's have none of your taciturn New England answers here. Explain yourself, if you will.'

Starlight nodded. 'When I found that Bright Town had been destroyed by the Night Witches, I took the last casket of Ice Dust that the people had hidden and set off in my boat to bring it here.'

'I know, I know,' Sir Chadwick interrupted. 'We received a message from the great bird that follows you around the world. We knew you were on your way.'

'I was coming,' Starlight continued, 'but I was attacked by two Shark Boats in the middle of the Atlantic Ocean.'

'A likely story,' Sir Chadwick replied. 'Had you encountered Shark Boats you wouldn't be here to tell us the tale.'

'I wouldn't be — but for the Ice Dust.'

'What do you mean?'

'I dipped my harpoons in it and when I speared the Shark Boats with them they exploded.'

'Nonsense!' said Sir Chadwick sharply. 'Ice Dust is only used for making Light Witch spells. It's an ingredient of magic — not an explosive.'

'Who told you that?' Starlight said.

Sir Chadwick shook his head. 'Well, that's the way it has always been.'

Starlight nodded vigorously. 'That's what we were taught to believe. But I made it work as an explosive.'

Sir Chadwick was silent for a while. Then he asked, 'How many Shark Boats have you sunk?'

'My count to date is fifty-nine,' Starlight replied. 'That's where all the Ice Dust has gone.'

'All gone?'

Starlight shrugged. 'I've a bit left — not much. I hoped

we might seek out a new mine in Antarctica which the
Night Witches have found.'

'A new mine!' Sir Chadwick was startled. 'You know of
another source of Ice Dust?'

'We do,' answered Starlight. 'My plan was to steal a
supply from them. But we've discovered there is a more
pressing problem.'

'And what is that, pray?'

'Bad news for you, I'm afraid. The Night Witches are
about to exterminate all Light Witches. Then they intend
to conquer the whole world.'

'Impossible,' Sir Chadwick said uneasily. 'They may
have temporarily defeated us, but their magic isn't powerful enough to actually kill us off. You're talking rubbish.'

'Am I?' Starlight said. 'You have a spy in the Night
Witch headquarters called Sally Oak?'

Sir Chadwick looked about him, agitated. 'You heard
Hilda Bluebell mention her when you were invisible.'

'Then how do we know she's been atomized?' Abby
interjected.

'Atomized?' Sir Chadwick repeated. 'And just what
does *atomized* mean?'

'This,' Abby replied and she held out her hand.

Sir Chadwick leaned forward and looked at the tiny
transparent cube in Abby's hand. Inside, he could see the
minute figure holding up her arms pleadingly. Sir Chadwick recoiled in horror. 'They did that to her?'

'That's right,' Abby answered. 'They may not be able to

kill you but they've found a way to imprison you all for eternity.'

Sir Chadwick shuddered. 'All eternity, poor Sally Oak.' He drew himself up, suddenly determined. 'We'll see about that. Now, what can we do?'

'Help us,' Starlight said. 'I can tell you how.'

The other Light Witches had gathered around the tiny cube containing Sally Oak. They turned to Sir Chadwick with frightened expressions in their eyes.

'Very well,' said Sir Chadwick, making his voice as confident as he could. 'You shall have the power of the Light Witches foursquare behind you.'

As he spoke, his nose suddenly began to grow to alarming proportions. Sir Chadwick clapped his hand to his face. 'That blasted sorcerer,' he gasped. 'He said there might be more side effects from his potion.'

'It doesn't look so bad from certain angles,' Spike said in an effort to be friendly.

Abby looked about her at the shabby theatre and Sir Chadwick's down-at-heel companions and the latest misfortune to blight the Master of the Light Witches. She didn't feel reassured.

Sir Chadwick and Hilda Restored

*A*part from Hilda Bluebell, Sir Chadwick dismissed the other Light Witches, who left the theatre. He led Starlight, Abby, Spike and Hilda, by the light of a lantern, to his dressing room which was backstage in the theatre.

'Sorry about the lack of electricity,' he said loftily. 'A temporary embarrassment over the bill.' The room they entered was crowded with dusty costumes, a collection of rickety old chairs and a sofa with broken springs that made a twanging sound when Abby and Spike sat down. Sir Chadwick lowered himself gently into a chair before the dressing-table and turned to them.

'Now, where do we begin?' he asked.

Abby handed him the scroll of blank parchment. 'There were words and a map on this,' she said. 'But it all faded away. Can you make them reappear?'

Sir Chadwick took the scroll and, with some difficulty, placed a pair of spectacles on the end of his enormous nose.

He peered over them at Abby. 'What happened when you took this?' he asked.

'There was a carved demon's head above it,' she explained. 'I thought it was made of wood, but when I took the map down from the wall the demon's head said, "The Curse of Mordoc upon you".'

Sir Chadwick sat back quickly and let the scroll fall to the floor. 'The Curse of Mordoc,' he repeated softly, gazing at the scroll with apprehension. 'That's a very powerful spell.'

'Can't you overcome it?' asked Starlight.

Sir Chadwick shook his head helplessly and pointed to his gigantic nose. 'Not in our present state. Our strength is almost gone.' He looked up and smiled ruefully. 'A diet of hot dogs is not really enough to maintain our special powers.'

'What do you need?' said Starlight.

'What we have lacked for so long,' Sir Chadwick said. 'Ice Dust.'

Starlight reached inside his pea jacket and produced a small leather bag. 'Is this enough?' he asked.

Sir Chadwick reached out, blinking in the light of the lantern, and took the bag. 'Hilda,' he said grandly. 'Bring out the ceremonial robes.'

Hilda opened a cupboard to reveal two other costumes. But Abby sighed with disappointment at the sight of them. Made of rough material like sackcloth, they were shapeless and moth-eaten. Small puffs of dust rose as Hilda took them from their pegs.

The two Light Witches carefully donned the robes, then

Sir Chadwick reached into the cupboard and produced a long wand with a silver cap at one end. He unscrewed it and with great care trickled a stream of Ice Dust into the hollow wand from the leather bag Starlight had given him.

Replacing the cap, he made several strokes through the air like a fencing master testing a rapier. Then, in a voice suddenly charged with authority he intoned:

'Ancient friends, what ere you be,
We call on thee to make us free.'

Immediately, Sir Chadwick's nose shrank to its normal size, and the scruffy robes began to glow with a strange white light. It grew stronger and stronger until it was so dazzling, that for a moment Abby had to cover her eyes. When she looked again, she gasped in astonishment.

Sir Chadwick and Hilda were now dressed in fantastic splendour. Hilda wore a long flowing white dress that seemed even lighter than silk. It was threaded with silver and gathered with clusters of pearls. Her face was quite beautiful. She had lost her pallor. Her long fair hair now framed her face in soft golden curls and was crowned with a silver tiara.

Sir Chadwick now looked immensely impressive. He seemed taller. His robe had been transformed into a long silken garment that swirled about his body.

Abby was reminded of the robe worn by the Master of the Night Witches. But Sir Chadwick's glittered with silver and the images that formed and flickered on it were of flowers and kindly smiling faces.

Sir Chadwick stooped down, picked up the parchment Abby had given him and handed it to Hilda. 'Hold this,' he commanded. Then he waved his wand.

Slowly, symbols and words began to reappear. Hilda lay the document on the dressing-table and they all gathered around it.

'What does it mean?' Abby asked.

Sir Chadwick shook his head and frowned. 'Very ancient. I think it is some kind of Icelandic language, but much older than anything I have ever encountered.' He looked up at Hilda. 'What do you suggest?'

'We shall have to consult the librarian, Master,' she replied.

Sir Chadwick groaned. 'And endure a lecture for our troubles, no doubt.' He shrugged. 'Well, there's no time to waste. Let's get on with it.' They returned their robes to the cupboard. 'Back to the stage,' Sir Chadwick instructed.

'Who is the librarian?' Abby asked as they hurried back through the theatre towards the stage.

'He's the keeper of all Light Witch records,' Sir Chadwick explained as he hurried ahead. 'Twenty millenniums of our history. Spell books, documents, biographies, written legends, folk law, recipes, he holds it all.'

'He must know a great deal,' said Spike.

'He does,' Hilda answered. 'But it hasn't improved his temper.'

Once more they stood upon the stage. 'Over here, everyone,' Sir Chadwick instructed. 'Stand as close to me as you can on this trapdoor, then hold hands with each other and close your eyes.'

Abby, Spike, Starlight and Hilda crowded against Sir Chadwick and he called out, 'Kavispol!' in a booming voice.

Just as she closed her eyes, Abby heard a very loud bang and saw the flash of an explosion. The floor seemed to give way beneath her feet. Down and down they plunged at breathtaking speed into pitch darkness.

The Saga of Mordoc's Land

Abby realised she had been holding her breath as they descended the deep dark shaft. She let it out with sudden force just as the platform began to slow down and they lurched to a stop.

'You can open your eyes now,' said Sir Chadwick.

The sight that greeted them astounded Abby and Spike.

'Great shark fins!' exclaimed Captain Starlight softly.

They were in a vaulted stone-flagged hall that was bigger than any cathedral. The ceiling was so high it was hardly visible in the gloom. As far as they could see in each direction, rows of bookshelves stretched into the distance.

A lone figure, seated at a long table piled with books, was writing with a quill pen in a large leather-bound ledger. He did not look up from his work as they approached. He was very thin with paper-white skin. A pair of eyeglasses rested on his long nose and he wore an old frock coat and a batwing collar. Even more extraordinary was his snow-white hair. It tumbled over his shoulders

and reached to the floor where it lay like pools of softly coiled silver.

'A hundred years has passed, Polartius. You need another haircut,' Sir Chadwick said in a jovial voice.

Abby and Starlight exchanged startled glances when they heard Sir Chadwick speak the librarian's name. Spike whispered, 'That's the name in your father's letter, Abby.'

The captain held a finger to his lips.

'I think you may be able to help us, Sir,' Abby said.

The old man ignored her. Without once raising his eyes, he flipped back through the ledger, ran a long thin finger down a list, then spoke in a high reedy voice. 'You're fifty-two years overdue with a copy of *Love Potions of the French Medieval Court*, Chadwick. You owe three thousand guineas in library fines.'

'I haven't got time for that now, Polartius,' Sir Chadwick said with a dismissive wave. 'Allow me to introduce my friends.'

'Don't bother,' the old man replied. 'I doubt if I shall ever see them again and I know enough people already. What do you want?'

'Can you translate this for us?' Sir Chadwick said, placing the scroll on the desk before him.

The old man reached out an ink-stained hand and held the scroll close to his nose.

'That's strange,' he sniffed. 'This document was stolen from our archives. How did it come into your possession?'

'The Night Witches had it.'

'Stolen, eh? Typical Night Witch behaviour.' Then he shook his head. 'I wonder how they got in here?'

'Never mind about that now, what do you make of it?'

'It's very early Icelandic.'

'We already know that,' Sir Chadwick snapped. 'What does it say?'

The old man shrugged. 'I can't remember the language. I haven't used it for at least a thousand years.'

'Can't you ask one of your elves?'

'They're having tea.'

'We'll wait.'

'Suit yourselves, but don't wander about.'

'May I remind you that I'm the Master of Light Witches,' Sir Chadwick said mildly.

'And I'm in charge of all these precious documents,'

snapped Polartius. 'You stick to your business and I will to mine.' And he returned to his ledger.

'May we have some seats?'

The old man made a gesture with his quill pen and suddenly a row of hard wooden chairs appeared behind them.

'Better humour him,' Sir Chadwick said in a low voice.

'Why must we wait for the elves, Sir Chadwick?' Abby asked. 'I thought you were the Master.'

'Only of Light Witches,' he answered. 'Elves are splendid chaps, if you're polite to them. But they hate their tea being interrupted.'

'Shssss!' the librarian said sharply and pointed with his pen to a sign bearing the word SILENCE which hovered above their heads. Like the chairs, Abby and Spike were sure it hadn't been there earlier.

They sat for quite a long time with only the sound of the quill pen scratching on the ledger. Abby was becoming very bored and Spike started to tap his foot but stopped immediately when the old man stared at him disapprovingly.

Then they heard a distant sound, like leaves rustling. Abby was sure it was laughter. She couldn't tell where they had came from but, suddenly, the space before the librarian's desk was filled with jolly little men who would only have come up to Abby's shoulder had she been standing up.

Like Polartius, they were dressed like Victorian gentlemen and were wearing shiny top hats. They gathered around Sir Chadwick, Starlight, Abby and Spike, cheerfully jingling the coins in their pockets.

'Hello, Sir Chadwick,' they sang out and waved in a friendly fashion.

'Did you enjoy your tea, gentlemen?' Sir Chadwick said in reply.

'Splendid,' called out one who was stouter than the rest. 'We had hot toasted buns with lots of butter and a chocolate cake.'

'We need a document translated,' Sir Chadwick said. 'It's early Icelandic.'

'I can do that,' replied the stoutest elf.

'Not here you can't,' said the librarian. 'Take them to your living room if you're going to chatter.'

'Ignore him,' whispered an elf. 'He's been in a bad mood since the Great Fire of London. Come this way.'

The elves went to one of the bookcases and pushed a section. It swung back to reveal a panelled room with a large marble fireplace, in which a log fire crackled. There were portraits of elves on the panelled walls and lots of old leather armchairs and sofas.

'Make yourselves comfortable,' the stout elf said. 'My name is Wooty, if Sir Chadwick is not going to introduce us.'

'Do forgive my bad manners,' Sir Chadwick said hurriedly, and he explained who everyone was.

'Captain Starlight, we've all heard of the Ancient Mariner. Nice to meet you Abby and Spike. We know Hilda, of course,' said Wooty brightly. 'Now, would you care for some tea? I could certainly do with another cup.'

'If it's no trouble.'

'None at all,' the little man answered and he rang a bell by the fireplace. A door opened and a stooped figure in a white coat entered.

'Tea again all round, please Charters,' Wooty ordered.

'The same order, sir?' the servant asked.

'Exactly the same, but there are four more now.'

A few moments later the white-coated figure reappeared with a massive silver tray heaped with buns, chocolate cake and sparkling china tea things. He placed it on the table before the fire.

'Shall I serve?' Charters asked.

'No, we'll help ourselves,' Wooty replied. 'Thanks all the same.' He picked up a teapot that seemed huge in his tiny hands and said, 'I'll be mother if you children would like to start on the buns,' and he handed Spike and Abby a long toasting fork each.

Only when they all had heaped plates and full cups did Wooty unroll the scroll.

'There's a map.'

'Is it of Antarctica?' Abby asked excitedly.

Wooty shook his head. 'No it's a map of an ancient Viking kingdom in the far north.'

'Oh,' said Abby.

'Cheer up,' said Starlight softly. 'Perhaps the words will tell us where to go.'

Wooty continued to examine the scroll. 'How interesting,' he said after a few moments. 'It's a vision story. You don't see many of them these days.'

'What does that mean?' asked Spike.

'Soothsayers used to tell legends from them around the ancient campfires. If you look into the flames of our fire you will be able to see the story as I read it.'

'I thought it was just a map,' Abby said.

'Oh, no, it's much more than that,' Wooty replied. 'Do you want me to begin?'

'When you're ready,' said Sir Chadwick.

Wooty gave a little cough and began to read in a much deeper voice:

'The epic of Turmec's journey to the Land of Mordoc.

'I am Votar, and what I tell you happened long ago. We were seafarers and our land was divided between Mordoc, who was an evil witch, and Turmec, who was good.'

They all looked into the fire as Wooty spoke and could see in the flickering flames the events he described.

'There was a great battle and Mordoc was defeated. He fled in his last ship, vowing to wreak his revenge.

'Turmec was a wise ruler but he wanted to explore beyond the horizons. One day, when he was gone on a long voyage, Mordoc returned.

'He had found great wealth and had hired another army and built more ships. He destroyed our village and our fleet. We few who survived waited in hiding until Turmec returned. He was filled with a terrible rage and, although he now only had one ship, he decided to pursue Mordoc.

'I was made part of the crew, as map-maker and keeper of the record. The voyage was hard. Great storms tore our sail and we rowed for long days until we had no more strength, nor water to drink. We prepared ourselves to die — but a strange craft that could fly through the heavens came down upon our boat.'

As Abby looked into the flames of the fire she could see an Atlantis Boat descending from the sky to settle on the becalmed sea next to Turmec's ship. She gripped Starlight's arm, but he held a finger to his lips when she was about to speak.

Wooty continued:

'The people, called Atlanteans, took us back to their city. Turmec told them of the evils of Mordoc and they gave him charts to copy that would help with our quest, and also a great crystal ball that could see through mist.

'The Atlanteans could speak to the whales, who told them that a great fleet of ships sailed out of a hidden land somewhere in the far south. So we voyaged to where the sea became ice. There we found strange birds that walked like men and flew beneath the sea instead of in the air.'

All of those gathered around the fire could see a great flock of penguins clustered together on an ice floe.

'The land we came to was as harsh. No trees or grass grew there and cliffs of ice guarded the shore. We found a bay but it was filled with Mordoc's ships, and we were only one.

'Turmec searched the coastline for another way into the land and finally we saw a mist formed on the ocean. We sailed into the fog and found whales basking in the waters. A warm river flowed into the sea. Turmec had found his way into the hidden land.

'Suddenly, we were caught in a mighty current. Turmec turned the vessel into the stream and we pulled on our oars against the force.'

Wooty stopped and drank some of his tea. 'Exciting, isn't it?' he said to his audience who were enthralled. 'Would you like me to go on, or would you like some more tea?'

'Go on!' they all chorused.

Wooty nodded and resumed his translation.

'The river flowed out of a tunnel through the ice cliffs. We pressed on until we saw a glowing light ahead. Suddenly, the vessel burst out of the tunnel and we found ourselves in a strange land.

'All was bathed in the same red light. The river was wider now, and the stream flowed more gently. Turmec moored the boat and we took stock of our surroundings.

'The air we breathed was warm and there was no sign of snow or ice. Strange plants grew all around us. We saw great ferns and trees with blossoms like white and golden trumpets. The hot moist air settled like dew on our brows. At first we thought there were birds in the sky, but they were butterflies the size of eagles.

'The strangest thing of all was the light. The source of it was two mountains tipped with fire. Turmec explained it to us. "The fire from those mountains warms the air. That is not the sky above us, but the ceiling of a great dome of ice. We are beneath it, in a New World."

'Turmec decided that we would continue to explore. The river did not flow in a straight line but meandered through the whole of the land. Sometimes, we came close to the edge of the great dome and could see the roof of ice. Then the river would turn again. In the centre of the land, a mighty storm of rain fell like a waterfall. All we could see was a mass of blueness obscuring all that existed beyond.

'More time passed and we came upon the place where the crews of Mordoc's Fleet had made a camp. We watched from a distance in the crystal eye, and saw they had fashioned dwellings from the great ferns that grew on the river bank. They had made the camp behind a high wall protected by sharp spikes, next to a road that led towards the centre of the land where the great rain fell.

'We also saw they had cut a tunnel and a great staircase in the ice wall of the dome, so wide that ten men abreast could walk up it at the same time. Turmec explained that it must have been the way to the bay where their fleet was anchored.

'We saw men hauling great sledges along the road. Each was piled high with precious gems. Diamonds, rubies and emeralds glittered in heaps. Mordoc had found a great treasure.

'But Turmec was puzzled. If the road and the river went to the same place, why did they not use the river to move their treasure?

'We continued along the river and came to a place where trees grew branches so low across the water they impeded our progress.

'Turmec ordered a man to stand at the prow of the vessel and hack our way through. Algrav was chosen, and just as we emerged from the worst of the thickets a fearful thing happened.

'A vast and terrible monster reared from the water ahead! The creature's body was black and covered with sores. It was as wide as our ship, but its head was more like that of a giant horned war-horse. When it opened its mouth we saw rows of jagged teeth and its eyes bulged with a fearsome madness.

'It thrust its great head forward and snapped Algrav into its mouth as a trout would a fly. Turmec drove our vessel on and we saw in the magic eye that the creature was resting beneath the sur-face of the river. It had the body of a giant eel but for two fins halfway along its length, and it was twice the length of our ship. Now we understood why Mordoc's crews had chosen to make a road. *They feared the creature in the river.*

'*A day passed and we did not see the great serpent again. I had almost finished my map. All that was left uncharted was the place of the great rains, which we now approached.*

'*The air was so filled with moisture and heat, the flowers and trees grew to an even greater height. At last, we saw the mighty wall of rain ahead, and beyond that lay the final mystery.*'

'Ohh!' Everyone sighed in disappoinment as the picture they were watching suddenly faded from the fire.

Wooty looked up. 'That's it,' he said. 'There is no more.'

'No more!' repeated Starlight. 'But surely there must be.'

'Perhaps there's a second document that has the rest of the story. Let's consult Polartius,' said Sir Chadwick. He turned to Wooty. 'Thank you for your help, gentlemen. If we find the second part we will ask you to continue with the translation.'

'You're most welcome,' said Wooty with a wave. 'Very nice to meet you all.'

Abby, Spike, Starlight and Hilda returned with Sir Chadwick to the librarian who looked up in disapproval at the motley collection once more gathered around his desk.

'There's a second part to this document, Polartius,' Sir Chadwick said.

'Yes, I know,' the old man replied.

'May we have it?'

'It's missing.'

'Missing?'

'That's what I said,' Polartius replied irritably. 'Obviously the Night Witch who stole the one you have in your possession must have the second part of the saga as well.'

Captain Starlight turned and addressed them all. 'We don't have time to return to the Night Witch headquarters to try and regain the missing part of the document. And they would probably be waiting for us in any case.'

'What shall we do?' asked Abby.

'Well, we know where we must head for the Land of Mordoc. At least we know some of the dangers we'll encounter when we get there. I say we press on,' Starlight said forcefully.

'A noble sentiment, my dear fellow,' said Sir Chadwick, clapping him on the back. 'We should prepare for the journey immediately.'

'You're coming with us?' Abby asked, incredulous.

'Of course,' replied Sir Chadwick. 'But there's just one piece of business I must take care of first.'

'I'm impressed by your attitude, Sir,' said Captain Starlight. 'I see I shall have to revise my opinion of English Light Witches.'

Sir Chadwick bowed at the compliment and Benbow, who had remained silent for so long, gave a loud squawk of approval.

Sir Chadwick
Stages a Play

With another sudden explosion and a cloud of smoke, the trapdoor on the stage of the Alhambra Theatre burst open and its passengers stepped from the platform that had transported them up from the library far below the streets of London.

Abby and Spike were yawning and feeling very sleepy.

'I think a good night's rest is needed by everyone,' said Sir Chadwick. 'My quarters are at your disposal, Captain Starlight. Come this way. You too, Hilda. I think it would be best if you stayed with us.'

They followed him behind the stage to a spiral staircase which led to an apartment high in the theatre. The living room was filled with overstuffed furniture. Memorabilia of the many parts Sir Chadwick had played cluttered the tables, the mantelpiece and the top of an upright piano.

There were daggers, a skull, a Persian slipper, pipes, a collection of revolvers, two Scottish swords, snuff boxes, and a marble bust of Napoleon. The walls were decorated with old posters and playbills. When they entered, a rather splendid, silver-haired figure was poking the fire that had just been lit.

'Shuffle, my butler,' Sir Chadwick said by way of introduction. 'You met his brother, Charters, who works for the elves. Shuffle, these people are my guests. Please prepare bedrooms for the children and Miss Bluebell. They wish to retire immediately. Captain Starlight and I will have a night-cap in here.'

'And what about the bird, Sir?' Shuffle replied, nodding towards Benbow, who was perched on the bust of Napoleon.

'Don't worry about Benbow,' Starlight said. 'Just open a window. He likes to sleep outside.'

'As you wish, Sir,' Shuffle said smoothly. 'And at what time will you require breakfast?'

'Seven o'clock sharp — and we shall want the full English version. None of your continental rolls and coffee,' said Sir Chadwick.

Shuffle coughed discreetly.

'Yes, what is it?' said Sir Chadwick.

'A question of finances, Sir. I fear our credit with the local shopkeepers is exhausted. In fact, they have become quite abusive of late.'

'Bring me my money suit,' Sir Chadwick said grandly.

Shuffle coughed again. 'I'm afraid it doesn't work any more, Sir. Don't you remember?'

'Just bring it to me, my dear fellow.'

Shuffle returned a moment later carrying another loud

check suit on a hanger. It also looked threadbare.

Sir Chadwick waved his wand and few sparkles of Ice Dust fell on the fabric. They all watched as the suit regained its full glory. 'Now look in the inside pocket,' instructed Sir Chadwick.

Shuffle did as he was told and withdrew a handful of bank notes.

'Will that do?'

'Admirably, Sir. Now can you do the same with the whisky?' He held up an empty decanter.

'I've got a better idea,' Sir Chadwick replied. 'Captain Starlight and I will pop along to Gerry's Club. It's time I settled my bar bill there.'

'Shall I wait up for you, Sir?'

'No, we shan't be long. Your evening's your own once you've seen to the others.'

'Thank you, Sir.'

'See you all at breakfast,' Sir Chadwick said. 'I'll just be a moment, Starlight, while I pop on my money suit.'

Abby was so tired she barely managed to stay awake while she washed her hands and face. The bed Shuffle showed her to was so comfortable she was asleep in an instant. During the night, she woke up and heard the sound of banging and loud laughter.

'Can you hear that, Spike?' she called out. He was just in the next room.

'I can now,' he replied. 'It's just Sir Chadwick and Captain Starlight singing a sea shanty. Go back to sleep.'

The next thing she knew, Shuffle had come into the room to draw the curtains. As he did so, Abby saw Benbow sitting on the windowsill outside. Shuffle opened the window and Benbow hopped into the room.

'May he have some breakfast too, please, Mr Shuffle?' Abby asked.

'And what would the bird care for, Miss? And the name's just Shuffle, by the way.'

'He likes fish cakes, Shuffle.'

'Salmon or cod?'

'Salmon, I think.' Benbow nodded in agreement.

'I have laid a table in the living room, Miss,' Shuffle announced in a soothing voice. 'Breakfast will be served in half an hour.'

Abby had a hot bath in Sir Chadwick's splendidly tiled bathroom and admired the gleaming brass taps and huge copper boiler.

When she returned to her bedroom she found her clothes had all been laundered and pressed.

Spike and Hilda Bluebell were already seated at the table when she entered. There was no sign of Starlight and Sir Chadwick. Shuffle entered with a steaming silver bowl. 'There's porridge to begin, if you wish it,' he announced. 'Or grapefruit. And there are eggs, bacon, sausages, kidneys and fried tomatoes in the dishes on the sideboard.'

'I think I'll have everything,' Spike said eagerly.

'No sign of Sir Chadwick and Captain Starlight yet?' Hilda Bluebell asked.

'Not yet, Miss. I understand they were delayed for longer than expected at Sir Chadwick's club.'

Hilda and the children had almost finished breakfast when Sir Chadwick eventually entered the room. He was unshaven, his hair was uncombed and he was wearing a long embroidered dressing gown. His eyes had a far away expression. Captain Starlight followed. They said nothing until Sir Chadwick raised his eyes from the tablecloth and said to Starlight.

'You're not wearing your cap.'

'My apologies,' Starlight replied stiffly and rose again. 'I shall get it immediately.'

While he was gone, Sir Chadwick said. 'I must say, the captain has a very fine singing voice.' He didn't speak again until he and Captain Starlight had drunk three large cups of coffee. Suddenly refreshed, Sir Chadwick cleared his throat and spoke to Hilda. 'Issue invitations to an extraordinary meeting of all the Light Witches for three o'clock this afternoon,' he instructed in an imperious manner.

'We'll never be able to get them here for three o'clock by writing to them, Master,' Hilda protested. 'I shall have to use the birds.'

'Do you know how to do that?' Sir Chadwick asked.

Hilda straightened her back. 'I read bird languages at Merlin College for my degree, Master. I can even speak Dodo, and that's a dead language.'

'I'm impressed, Hilda. Summon your feathered friends, if you please.'

She went to the window and clapped her hands four times. There was a momentary pause, then came the sound of thousands of beating wings. Suddenly, the sky outside the windows was filled with a great flock of whirling starlings. Hilda flung the windows wide open and began to whistle exactly like a bird.

When she'd shut the window again, Spike asked, 'What was that you said to them, Hilda?'

'A rough translation would be:

'Feathered friends whose hearts are free,
Bring all Light Witches here to me.
This request they shall not mock,
I want them here at three o'clock.'

They saw the flock of starlings swoop in a great circle, then they were gone.

Sir Chadwick turned to the others. 'Now, what about provisions for our expedition?'

Captain Starlight lifted his cap and scratched his head. 'We've got some ship's biscuits and a good strong cheese, and plenty of Boston baked beans. I dare say we could load a few cans of pickled herrings.'

Sir Chadwick shuddered. 'I shall be rather busy this morning. Perhaps you could go to Fortnum & Mason in Piccadilly. They know me there. Give them this.' He handed Starlight a card. 'Tell them to make up a hamper in my name, with enough supplies for all of us for as long as you think fit.' He paused for a moment. 'How shall we be travelling?'

'In our Atlantis Boat,' Abby answered.

'A sea voyage — splendid! I shall require a port cabin and accommodation for Shuffle.'

'We're a bit cramped to take Shuffle as well,' Captain Starlight pointed out.

Sir Chadwick didn't seem at all bothered. 'I'm afraid you'll have to stay behind, Shuffle.'

'I shall endeavour to contain my disappointment, Sir.'

'Good, good,' said Sir Chadwick. 'Now remember, Captain, be back here by one o'clock sharp, after you've loaded the supplies on board.'

Starlight thought for a moment. 'I can do the shopping on my own,' he said. 'Why don't you children do some sightseeing while you're in London? Perhaps Sir Chadwick can spare Miss Bluebell to escort you.'

'Yes, yes,' said Sir Chadwick in a preoccupied manner. 'As long as she's back by one o'clock.'

'What are you going to do?' Starlight asked.

Sir Chadwick drummed on the table with his fingertips. 'Make arrangements to expose a traitor in our midst,' he answered.

'How will you do that, Master?' Hilda asked.

'I'm working on a plan even as we speak,' said Sir Chadwick.

Hilda Bluebell took her duties as a guide seriously. By half-past twelve, Abby and Spike had seen the Tower of London, Buckingham Palace, the British Museum, the Natural History Museum, the Science Museum and Regent's Park

Zoo. They had zigzagged about the city by underground train, on the tops of buses and in the back of taxis.

'Oh, dear,' she said finally, as they stood on the steps of the National Gallery in Trafalgar Square. 'We have to be back at the theatre in fifteen minutes and we've masses to see yet.'

'I don't really mind,' Spike said wearily.

'Well, we'd better walk back,' Hilda said. 'It's not very far.'

They set off at a brisk pace and were soon back in Shaftesbury Avenue. As they approached the Alhambra Theatre, Abby and Spike gasped at the transformation that had taken place. The theatre sparkled in the bright autumn sunshine. There were new posters and the sign above proclaimed:

SIR CHADWICK STREET PRESENTS

by invitation only

A special matinee performance of

PETER PAN

by J. M. Barrie

Starring

Sir Chadwick Street as *Captain Hook*

Hilda Bluebell as *Peter Pan*

Abby Clover as *Wendy*

Spike Lostboy as *Nana*

'Oh, dear,' said Hilda. 'I've got to wear that flying costume again. I was hoping the part of Peter would go to someone else.'

'What's the flying costume?' Spike asked.

'You'll see,' Hilda replied as she hurried them into the theatre.

Abby was deeply puzzled. 'I thought Sir Chadwick was looking for a traitor,' she said. 'Why is he putting on a play just as we're all about to leave?'

'I can only suppose he has a good reason,' Hilda answered.

When Spike and Abby entered the stalls, the stage was in chaos. Sir Chadwick stood, dressed in the costume of Captain Hook, shouting directions above the banging of hammers as stage hands moved furniture and adjusted scenery to construct the nursery bedroom of the Darling family.

'Where are the children?' he bellowed.

'Here, Master,' Hilda called out.

'Excellent,' shouted Sir Chadwick. 'Abby is to play Wendy and Spike the dog, Nana. We can borrow two of the elves for the parts of John and Michael and the rest of them can play the lost boys.'

'But I can't play Wendy,' Abby said anxiously. 'I don't know the part.'

'You will when I direct you, child,' Sir Chadwick answered confidently. 'The cast is to assemble on stage in ten minutes.

We shall have a full dress performance in half an hour.'

As the noise grew louder a woman in the orchestra pit reached up to tug at the hem of Sir Chadwick's coat. He looked down at her for a moment and held a hand to his ear, but could not hear what she was saying. Finally, he shouted, 'Stop!' in a voice that boomed to the back of the theatre.

There was a sudden silence.

'Who are you and what do you want?' Sir Chadwick demanded.

'Don't you remember, Master, I'm Clara Parsley. You appointed me theatre manager just an hour ago,' she replied.

'Of course you are, my dear,' Sir Chadwick said. 'And a splendid job you're doing. Now what is the problem?'

Clara looked down at the clipboard she carried. 'The theatre hasn't been cleaned for years. There are wasp nests in two of the boxes, three rows of seats are broken and half of the house lights don't work.'

Sir Chadwick sighed. 'Has anyone seen my wand?' he asked. A passing stagehand picked it up from where it was lying in the wings and gave it to him.

Sir Chadwick frowned for a moment, then with a wave of his wand, shouted:

'Spirit of Avon, help our story.
Restore your home to her former glory.'

Sparks of Ice Dust flew from the tip of his wand and, as if they had a life of their own, darted into the gloomiest recesses of the theatre. Like a painting that had been stripped of a layer of dark varnish, the grubby interior was suddenly restored to all its original splendour.

Great chandeliers sparkled with light which glinted on the gold mouldings that embossed the curve of the circle and the boxes. The plush of the upholstered seats glowed rose-red once again and the dark blue carpets looked newly laid.

There was a sudden loud bang from the trapdoor on the stage and a pyramid of elves arrived from the depths of the library. Like a team of well-dressed acrobats, the elves tumbled on to the stage.

'All cast members stand in a tight group,' Sir Chadwick instructed. 'I only want to perform this spell once.'

Everyone shuffled together and Sir Chadwick watched them carefully.

'Squeeze together now,' he instructed. Then he waved

his wand and called out:

'Forget yourselves, let minds be free,
Actors now is what you'll be.
Don't say you can't, just say you can,
You are the cast of Peter Pan.
In your mind you'll know the part,
But heed that acting's from the heart.'

Abby could feel the tiny particles of Ice Dust sprinkle over her. For a moment, it tingled like pins and needles.

'All to wardrobe now,' Sir Chadwick shouted. 'Five minutes to change and then back on stage.'

Abby followed the others and was directed to the dressing room she was to share with Hilda. There she found a long wig and a Victorian nightdress ready for her.

Hilda helped her with her make-up and the harness she had to wear so she could fly on the stage wires. She looked at herself in a long mirror when it was finished and was quite pleased with the result.

'I suppose I'd better get into mine,' Hilda said with a sigh, as she reached into a cupboard and pulled out a large cardboard box that quivered as though there was something alive inside.

'Now, behave yourself,' she said sharply. As she lifted the lid a Peter Pan costume flew out of the box and hovered before them as though it were being worn by an invisible figure.

'No tricks now,' Hilda said, addressing the costume as she plucked various items out of the air and quickly began to dress.

'Why don't we all have a flying costume like yours?' Abby asked enviously.

Hilda placed the little feathered hat on her head before she answered. 'Sir Chadwick made this one after a long lunch at his club,' Hilda explained. 'He was a bit tired and he didn't get it quite right. Sometimes the costume has a mind of its own. It's not wicked – just a bit mischievous, like the real Peter Pan. Sir Chadwick decided not to risk it with the other costumes.'

There was a knock on the door and a voice called out, 'On stage now, everybody.' Abby took a deep breath and suddenly began to feel very nervous.

The Ordeal of the Tickling Elves

A bby found Spike in the wings, dressed in his dog costume. He was peering through a peephole in the curtains. 'The whole theatre is full,' he said excitedly. 'But I still haven't seen Captain Starlight. He's not in his seat in the box.'

Abby felt distinctly nervous. She didn't know how she was going to perform.

Just then, Sir Chadwick appeared. Abby watched him mutter something to Hilda, then turn to the rest of the cast and say, 'Positions everyone,' in a louder voice. A sudden calmness came over Abby. Somehow, she knew exactly what she had to do. The curtain rose and there was a murmur of pleasure from the audience when they saw the Darling family's nursery.

For Abby, everything was a new and wonderful experience. She had never seen a performance of *Peter Pan* before, so the story unfolded as though it was actually happening to her. She spoke her lines almost without thinking, as if they had just come into her head.

Between scenes, Sir Chadwick saw her in the wings and recognised the expression on her face. 'You look stage-struck, child,' he said in a kindly voice.

'It's wonderful — just like...' she was suddenly lost for words.

'Magic?' he answered with a wry smile.

'More magical than anything I've ever known,' agreed Abby. 'Even more than being able to disappear. Is it always like this on the stage, Sir Chadwick?'

'Always for me, child,' he said softly.

When the cast had taken their bows and the final curtain fell, the Light Witch audience rose to its feet with shouts of 'Bravo! Bravo!' The applause echoed around the auditorium as Sir Chadwick strode to the front of the stage and held up his hand.

'Ladies and gentlemen and fellow members of the ancient order of Light Witches, please take your seats.'

There was a ripple of conversation in the auditorium and Sir Chadwick held up his hand for silence.

'I'm afraid our pleasure in giving this performance — and your gratifying response — must be spoilt by something I have to reveal to you all...' He paused dramatically, then said, 'There is a traitor in our midst.'

Once again there was a loud muttering from the audience.

'Please be silent a moment longer,' Sir Chadwick continued. 'This person, who is acting for the Night Witches, has removed a valuable document from our library and passed vital information to the enemy.'

Sir Chadwick now held up both his arms in triumph. 'The good news is, we have identified this traitor and I am now able to reveal to you all who that person is.'

He pointed an accusing finger towards the third row in the stalls, at an individual sitting by the aisle. 'It is you, Sir!' he roared in a thunderous voice.

A tall figure with a long crooked nose and wild curling black hair rose to his feet and attempted to run from the theatre. But he was overcome by several of the elves who had crept up on him while Sir Chadwick had been speaking.

'Bring him on to the stage,' commanded Sir Chadwick.

'I am Cosmo Nettlebed, and I am innocent. *Innocent!*' the tall figure shouted as the elves led him to Sir Chadwick.

Abby was amazed. '*Nettlebed!* He was the deck hand on Captain Starlight's boat with my mother and father,' she whispered to Spike. 'He must have known Polartius and come here to steal the map. That's how the Night Witches knew where to go in Antarctica.'

Spike nodded, but was trying to follow what was happening on the stage.

'I am innocent. Innocent!' Nettlebed continued to shout.

'Silence,' Sir Chadwick thundered. 'I have undeniable proof of your guilt, Nettlebed.'

'I demand to know what it is,' the tall figure answered.

'Who are you to make demands of me, Sir?'

'I have as much right to speak as you have. I am a first class Light Witch,' shouted Nettlebed.

'We'll see about that,' Sir Chadwick replied and looked over his shoulder into the wings. 'Where is my Peter Pan?' he called out.

'Up here, Master,' Hilda answered.

And all eyes turned to the high ceiling where she was clinging to one of the great chandeliers.

'What on earth are you doing up there?' asked Sir Chadwick. 'Come down at once.'

'I can't, Master,' Hilda replied. 'The costume won't let me.'

Sir Chadwick shook his fist. 'Costume, I've warned you about this sort of behaviour before. I won't tolerate it any longer.' He waved his wand and shouted:

'Costume of my own creation,
You must learn your proper station.
No more silly tricks you'll play,
Bring down Hilda right away.'

When he had completed the spell, Hilda let go of the chandelier and the costume flew her in a lazy circle down to the stage. Sir Chadwick took her hand and said, 'Now tell the audience what instructions I gave you before the performance.'

Hilda faced the Light Witches. 'Sir Chadwick said I had a very special duty to perform during the scene where Tinker Bell was in danger of dying.'

Sir Chadwick stepped forward. 'Ladies and gentlemen, we are all familiar with the moment in the play where Peter

Pan flies over the auditorium and urges the audience to clap
if they want to save Tinker Bell's life, are we not?'

'Of course, of course,' the audience replied.

'And what did this wretch do during that vital
moment?' Sir Chadwick asked Hilda as he pointed to
the prisoner.

'He didn't clap, Master.'

A gasp of outrage rose from the audience.

Sir Chadwick held up his hands. 'What further evidence
do you need?' he shouted. 'A Light Witch who wouldn't
clap to save the life of Tinker Bell!'

'I deny the charge,' Cosmo Nettlebed shouted.

'So you still refuse to admit you are secretly a Night
Witch?' Sir Chadwick demanded.

'I do,' howled Nettlebed.

Sir Chadwick drew himself up to his full height. 'Then
you leave me no alternative. As Master of the Light
Witches, I sentence you to trial by ordeal. If you are a
Light Witch then the punishment I prescribe will hardly
cause you any discomfort. But if you are a Night Witch, the
shame and humiliation will be an agony to you.' Sir Chadwick paused dramatically. 'I sentence you to be tickled by
elves.' There was another gasp from the audience.

'Why is that so terrible?' Abby asked Hilda who stood
beside her in the wings. 'Being tickled by elves doesn't
sound so bad to me.'

'That's because you're not a Night Witch,' Hilda
replied. 'Night Witches can't bear to look silly. Their pride

makes it agony for them and they only laugh when something horrible happens to somebody else. If they laugh
under any other circumstances, each chuckle ages them by
a year. If Nettlebed is a Night Witch then he would rather
have a long hot bath than be tickled by elves.'

'Let the sentence begin,' Sir Chadwick pronounced
solemnly. The elves surrounding Nettlebed now began
their task. Two of them removed his shoes and socks and
produced feathers from their pockets; others ran their tiny
hands beneath his coat, seeking his ribs.

For almost a minute, Nettlebed struggled but remained
silent. Then he could contain himself no longer. A long
snigger escaped from his curled lips, then a chortle and
finally an explosive bellow of laughter. The laughter continued as the elves went on with their work.

Nettlebed's black hair began to turn a dirty grey as each
laugh escaped from his convulsed and twisting body. His
crooked nose grew even longer and, gradually, his skin
turned parchment white and his hands became withered
and claw-like.

'Enough,' called out Sir Chadwick eventually. 'Bring a
looking glass.'

A large mirror was carried on to the stage and set
before Cosmo Nettlebed. When he saw his reflection he let
out a scream of rage. 'Damnation on you all,' he cried out.
'The Curse of Mordoc on you!'

'Your curse will do no good here, Nettlebed. Your
powers are almost gone,' Sir Chadwick replied.

'My powers may have waned,' Nettlebed replied with a final flicker of defiance. 'But you're all doomed – all of you Light Witches. We have captured the Ancient Mariner. Captain Adam Starlight won't be able to help you any more.'

'Where have you taken him?' Sir Chadwick demanded.

'To a secret place – even I don't know where – so you won't be able to get that information from me,' Nettlebed said triumphantly.

'Take him away,' Sir Chadwick instructed. 'Have his name struck from the great book of Light Witches.' He turned once more to the audience.

'Ladies and gentlemen, thank you for your time and cooperation. If you will now kindly leave the theatre, I will keep you posted on future developments.'

Abby and Spike had approached Sir Chadwick. 'What shall we do about Captain Starlight?' Abby asked.

'Stay calm,' he replied in a commanding voice. 'First, go and change out of your costumes and then meet me in my quarters.'

Before Abby left the stage she looked about the auditorium, seeking a familiar shape, but there was no sign of Benbow.

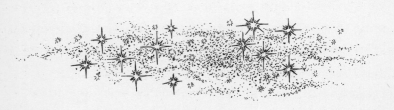

Love Finds Sir Chadwick Street

When Abby and Spike knocked on the door of Sir Chadwick's living room, they could hear the sound of a songbird. The sound continued as his voice called out, bidding them to enter. Once they were inside the living room, Abby and Spike saw that the birdsong was coming from Hilda.

'First class, Hilda. That was delightful. I must say you really know your subject. Now, this is what I want you to do. We know that Captain Starlight set out for Fortnum & Mason in Piccadilly. On route he disappeared. Find out if the birds have seen anything unusual that may give us a clue to his whereabouts.'

'May I use this window, Master?' Hilda asked, pointing across the room.

'Help yourself,' he replied. 'And I'll have Shuffle prepare us a high tea. I had to miss luncheon because of the performance.'

Hilda opened the window and began to chirrup loudly,

then she changed to a cooing sound, and finally to a fluting whistle. After a few moments, the window-sill was crowded with birds and many others clouded the sky. All of them seemed to be communicating with Hilda. Eventually, she turned back to Sir Chadwick. 'Two pigeons seem to have seen something, Master. May I ask them inside?'

'By all means.'

The great flocks of birds dispersed as the two fat pigeons hopped over the window-sill. They stood on the table and began to coo urgently. Hilda translated.

'They say they saw a man in a sailor's cap loading hampers into a taxi in Piccadilly. A big white bird was perched on top of Burlington Arcade, watching him.'

'That would be Benbow,' Spike interrupted.

Sir Chadwick held up a hand. 'Go on.'

The pigeons continued to coo and Hilda translated. 'As he put the last hamper in to the taxi, four figures in black cloaks appeared. They conjured up a strange dusty cloud that enveloped the man. He seemed to fall down. Then the cloud thickened and hid them from sight. When the wind blew the foul cloud away, they had all vanished.'

'Perhaps they have taken him to Night Witch headquarters,' Abby suggested in the silence that followed.

Hilda shook her head. 'I think some of the other birds would have seen that.'

'Did they see Benbow again?' Sir Chadwick asked.

Hilda cooed to the pigeons. They shook their heads. She thanked them and they flew off through the window.

She was about to close it again when she noticed something high in the sky. The dot grew bigger and they could see it was Benbow. He entered the room and perched on the mantelpiece.

'Does he know where the Night Witches have taken Captain Starlight?' Sir Chadwick said.

'I'm afraid I can't speak albatross, Master. It's a secret language,' Hilda replied.

Benbow hopped over to an old typewriter on the sideboard. He tapped a key with his beak and then looked towards Abby.

'Please put some paper in the machine, Sir Chadwick,' she requested.

He did as she asked and Benbow tapped quickly with his beak.

'Lost Land!' said Sir Chadwick. 'Oh, dear,' he said softly. 'That is bad news.'

'Where's Lost Land?' said Spike. 'Can't we follow them there?'

Sir Chadwick nodded. 'Oh, we could. That's exactly what they want us to do. They must be setting a trap.'

'What kind of a trap?' asked Spike.

'It's easy to go to the Lost Land. It's getting back that can be difficult,' Sir Chadwick explained.

'How difficult?' said Abby.

'You have to be sure someone loves you so much they will want to see you again more than anything else in the whole world.'

'That's easy,' said Abby. 'I know my mum and dad love me that much.'

'What about me?' Spike asked.

Abby turned to him. 'Aunt Lucy and Uncle Ben love you, Spike.'

'Are you sure?'

'Quite sure.'

'Well, I'm all right then,' Spike said with a grin.

'We can't all go,' Sir Chadwick said.

'Why not?' asked Abby.

Sir Chadwick took the pouch from his pocket and shook it. 'We don't have much Ice Dust left. We will have to ration it very carefully. There's another hitch as well.'

'What's that?' asked Spike.

Sir Chadwick slumped down in a chair. 'I will have to go with you — the problem is, I don't think there is any-one in the world who loves me that much.'

'No one?' Abby said sympathetically.

Sir Chadwick shook his head sadly. 'I've had no time for romantic attachments in my life. Always busy in the theatre — and being Master of the Light Witches has taken up the rest of my time.'

There was a silence and they all looked at the floor. Then Hilda cleared her throat. When Abby looked at her she could see that Hilda was bright red. 'I love you, Mas-ter,' she said in a whisper.

Sir Chadwick shook his head. 'Admiration is not the

same as love, child — if only it were.'

'No,' Hilda said in a stronger voice. 'I really love you.'

Sir Chadwick looked startled. 'But our ages, you're just a young girl, I'm... well, I'm...'

'You're thirty-two in Light Witch years, Master,' Hilda said in a sudden firm voice. 'Only seven years older than me — and that's a very lucky number.'

Sir Chadwick looked nonplussed. 'Are you sure?'

Hilda sighed. 'You keep thinking you're older than you are because you were such a big hit as the old father in *King Lear*. That's why I keep urging you to do a production of *Romeo and Juliet*. Romeo was only eighteen. It might reset your time clock.'

'Wouldn't I be too young for you then?'

'Not if I were to play Juliet,' Hilda answered. 'She was only fourteen.'

'And you *really* love me?'

'Of course.'

Sir Chadwick took her hand and kissed it. 'My Juliet!'

'I hope this doesn't go on for much longer,' Spike said to Abby in a loud whisper. 'And anyway, what are Light Witch years?'

Sir Chadwick turned to Spike. 'Human beings age twenty years for every Light Witch year.'

Abby gasped and did a rapid sum in her head — she was good at arithmetic. 'But that makes you six hundred and forty years old!'

'Quite right,' Sir Chadwick replied. Then he turned to

Spike. 'And you're right too, young man. Our personal lives must take second place to the duty we must perform. We have important work to do.'

'That's my favourite kind of work,' said Spike.

Sir Chadwick leaned against the mantelpiece. 'Hilda, my child — I mean, my love — you must make fairy threads for Abby, Spike and myself and one for Starlight — when we find him. Attach Starlight's thread to something I can put in my pocket.' There was a gentle squawk from Benbow. 'I apologise. Make a thread for Benbow as well, please, Hilda.'

'What are fairy threads?' asked Abby.

Sir Chadwick turned to her. 'The threads are made from specks of Ice Dust. They stretch as far as you want them to go. They're so fine, there was an old saying that only fairies could see them.'

'So they're as thin as a spider's gossamer?' asked Abby.

'Oh, much finer,' Sir Chadwick replied, leaning for a moment on the bust of Napoleon. 'And they are very difficult to manufacture. Men nearly always make them too thick.'

'What do we do with them?' Abby asked.

Sir Chadwick drummed his fingers on the top of Napoleon's head for a moment. 'We tie them to ourselves. Then when we want to get home we simply think of someone who loves us and pull ourselves back to safety.'

'Why will we have to do that?'

'The Lost Land is not of this world,' Sir Chadwick explained. 'It's the place where things go when their owners lose them. Once we're there, it would be easy for us to get lost ourselves.'

'I'm not sure I understand,' said Abby.

Sir Chadwick thought for a moment. 'Did you ever have a toy that you neglected to look after, then when you wanted it again, you couldn't find it — no matter how hard you looked?'

'Yes,' said Abby after a moment of thought.

Sir Chadwick stood up and made a circular motion in the air. 'Well, in all probability, it is now in the Lost Land. We all have past possessions there. But, as I said, it's not really of this world. So, if we visit, we tie fairy threads to ourselves. That way we can pull ourselves back when we want to return.'

'I think I understand,' Abby said, even though she was still quite puzzled.

'Well I don't,' Spike said sadly. 'I can't remember anything I ever lost — or anything I ever had, come to that.'

Sir Chadwick nodded thoughtfully. 'Yes, there could be complications in your case, my boy. I think on reflection it would be better if you stayed behind.'

'I don't mind going,' Spike said eagerly.

'I know, I know,' Sir Chadwick said, holding up a hand. 'But it might endanger the rest of us and you wouldn't want to do that, would you?'

'Not for anything,' said Spike, reluctantly accepting

Sir Chadwick's decision.

While Hilda worked, Abby practised whistling the tune that made her disappear, and Sir Chadwick sat in an armchair dozing by the fire. Benbow also took a nap. He sat on the bust of Napoleon and folded his head beneath his wing.

Eventually, Hilda stood up and said, 'Right, the threads are ready.' She held up four rings. 'Master, if you and Abby and Benbow put these on now, you can put the ring for Starlight in the waistcoat pocket of your money suit. When you find him, remember to put it on his finger.'

Benbow held out his leg and Hilda slipped on his ring, then she handed the others to Abby and Sir Chadwick.

'A beautiful job,' Sir Chadwick said, holding out his hands. 'Quite invisible.'

Abby waved the hand on which she wore the ring through the air. All she could feel was the slightest tugging. 'It doesn't feel very strong,' she said.

'No one knows just how strong a fairy thread actually is,' said Sir Chadwick. 'But there is a record of three Light Witches bringing an elephant back from the Lost Land. And all they used was a single thread.'

'How could anyone forget an elephant?' asked Spike.

Sir Chadwick looked slightly uncomfortable. 'I was very busy at the time, rehearsing a new play,' he said, standing up. 'I had a great deal on my mind.' He looked embarrassed and dusted down his trousers. 'Now I think we should be on our way.'

'So how do we actually get there?' said Abby.

'Well, first we have to get lost,' said Sir Chadwick opening the window again. 'We'll see you down in the street, Benbow.'

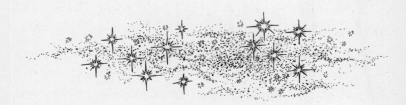

Journey into the Unknown

Afew minutes later, Sir Chadwick, Abby and Benbow were standing in Shaftesbury Avenue. Sir Chadwick hailed a taxi. 'I'm only going east, guv,' the driver grunted as Sir Chadwick leaned down towards the cab window.

'Splendid,' Sir Chadwick answered. 'The East End is a complete mystery to me. Are you familiar with it, Abby?'

'This is my first time in London,' she replied.

'What about you, Benbow, do you know the East End?'

Benbow shook his head.

Sir Chadwick turned back to the driver. 'Where do you live, cabbie?'

'Forty-six Paint Lane, Whitechapel.'

'Take us there,' said Sir Chadwick opening the door.

'It'll be extra for that bird,' the taxi driver said grumpily, nodding towards Benbow.

'Money is no object,' Sir Chadwick replied. 'Now, please make haste.'

The taxi driver shrugged and pulled away into the traffic.

'Everyone close your eyes,' Sir Chadwick instructed. 'We mustn't know the route to where we are going.'

With eyes tightly shut, they rattled through the streets of London until the taxi finally shuddered to a halt.

'Paint Lane,' the cabbie announced.

They got out of the taxi into a narrow, deserted, cobbled road lined with terraced brick houses. It was raining gently and somewhere a clock was chiming the hour.

'Just as I imagined it,' said Sir Chadwick, looking about him at the dismal scene. 'Pity there's no fog.'

'We haven't had fog around here since 1961,' the cabbie snarled. He grabbed the money from Sir Chadwick's hand, strode over to enter number forty-six and slammed the door behind him.

'What a disagreeable fellow,' Sir Chadwick said. 'I think I might bring some fog back from the Lost Land for him, if we have the time.'

'What do we do now?' Abby asked.

'We must all close our eyes again and think of something we lost, long ago, and wish we had it back. Do you understand Benbow?'

The great bird nodded.

'Now you two start thinking,' said Sir Chadwick.

Abby remembered a wooden horse she had once owned. She thought so hard she could remember the little red wheels on the base.

'Remember harder,' called out Sir Chadwick and his

voice sounded far away.

Suddenly, Abby heard a rushing sound and felt as though she were being pulled through a long, narrow tube. When she put out her hands, the sides of the tube were as soft and smooth as velvet. Then there was a sudden popping sound and she felt firm ground beneath her feet once more.

'Welcome to the Lost Land,' Sir Chadwick said. 'You can open your eyes now.'

Temptations of
The Lost Land

Abby gasped at the sight that greeted her. She and Sir Chadwick were standing on the peak of a sand dune. A seemingly endless desert of golden sand stretched out to the horizon on all sides of them. The sun blazed down from a dazzling blue sky. High above, Benbow circled. Abby was wearing her Atlantis coat but, strangely, she didn't feel at all warm.

'I didn't expect this,' she said.

'It won't last for long,' Sir Chadwick said. 'Come on.'

'How do you know which way to go?' Abby asked.

Sir Chadwick shrugged. 'It doesn't matter which way you go in the Lost Land,' he answered. 'We want to find Captain Starlight so eventually we shall come to him.'

'How can you be so sure?'

Sir Chadwick stopped. 'Because we want to. I keep forgetting you've not been here before,' he said. 'Now this is very important. Under no circumstances must you touch anything you recognise — or speak to anyone who seems familiar from your past.'

'Why not?' said Abby.

'That's the way the Night Witches keep you here,' Sir Chadwick explained. 'They made the Lost Land to capture people with their regrets. If you see something you once possessed and want to have it again, the moment you touch it, you're trapped here for ever. Imagination becomes a terrible reality.'

'But it's real now.'

'Is it?' said Sir Chadwick. 'Then why aren't you hot? He pointed to the sky. 'The sun should be burning us.'

'I wondered about that,' Abby replied.

'That's because you're experiencing somebody else's lost day, not your own. Maybe it was an Arab boy or girl who wasted it, and now they're sorry they didn't take advantage when they had the chance. Just remember that everything changes all the time here. So many people waste so many days.'

They took another few paces and found themselves on a high mountain path. It was winter and snow was falling. 'Do you see what I mean?' said Sir Chadwick.

'It's very confusing,' replied Abby.

'Typical Night Witch work. Keep going.'

They walked on and, as Sir Chadwick had predicted, the scenery continued to change. One moment they were in a rain forest where brightly coloured tropical birds flitted through the trees. Then they were crossing a great plain of high grass, while a thunderstorm filled the air with sheet lightning.

Suddenly, a seaside beach stretched before them. There was a pier where a brass band played. Abby blinked and then they were walking at night through the streets of a beautiful city where all the traffic was pulled by horses. Next, they were on a cliff top on a summer's morning. Abby recognised where she was. It was the path to the cove above Speller. She felt wonderfully happy. 'I'm home,' she called out. Then she saw the little wooden horse she had remembered. It was lying in the long grass next to the path and Abby could hear her aunt calling her name.

'Aunt Lucy,' Abby shouted. 'I'm here,' and she leaned down to pick up her lost toy.

Sir Chadwick pulled her away roughly and clapped his hand over her mouth. 'It's a trap, Abby,' he whispered, darting a furtive glance over his shoulder. 'Now the Night Witches know we are here. They would have heard your voice.'

'How do you know?' she whispered.

'I just saw my favourite tavern. Old friends were calling me from the doorway.'

'I didn't see it.'

'That's how it is,' Sir Chadwick replied. 'I didn't see what you were reaching for. But I knew it was something you wanted. We must be very close to Starlight. The traps are coming thick and fast.'

They took a few more steps and the scene changed again. They were now in gently rolling countryside and it was a spring day. The lane they were strolling along was lined with low hedgerows. On each side there were small fields, some with crops growing, and others holding herds of cows or flocks of sheep. As they approached a farm-house, a cock crowed and Abby saw a plump farmer's wife standing in a doorway, wiping her hands on her apron.

'Come in, girl, and have a glass of buttermilk,' the woman called out in the same accent as Captain Starlight's.

'Don't look,' Sir Chadwick instructed. 'We must be in the New England Starlight lost. He will be very close to us – and so will the Night Witches.'

They came to the brow of a hill and just on the other side was an old oak tree close to the side of the lane. On the grassy bank, beneath the shade of its spreading branch-es, Captain Starlight lay sleeping peacefully.

Benbow was sitting beside him. The lane curved down to a cove where a little town of wooden houses with shingle roofs nestled next to the sea. Sailing ships lined the small jetty and wisps of smoke curled from the chimneys. It was very beautiful.

'Bright Town,' Sir Chadwick said in a gentle voice. 'This is how it was before it was destroyed. The Night Witches have been very cunning.'

'Can't we just slip the ring on his finger and all go back now?' Abby asked. Despite the peacefulness of the scene, she was feeling decidedly uneasy.

Sir Chadwick shook his head. 'No, we have to be very careful. This is some sort of trap.'

'How can you tell?'

'I know the way the Night Witch mind works. If Starlight wakes up, he won't know he's in the Lost Land. And if he responds to a familiar voice or touches something he'll be done for — marooned in the Lost Land for ever.'

'What can we do?' said Abby.

Sir Chadwick began to search frantically through the pockets of his suit. 'Ah,' he said eventually, and produced a curious object.

Abby could not make out what it was at first.

'My old *Richard III* nose,' Sir Chadwick said. 'It's made of soft wax.'

'What will you do with it?'

'We have to be very careful not to wake him,' Sir Chadwick explained. 'While he is still asleep we must blindfold him and block up his ears. Now, lift up his head — be gentle.'

As Abby slowly raised Starlight's head, Sir Chadwick took off his flowing bow tie and quickly tied it over the sleeping Captain's eyes. Then he pulled the false nose into two pieces and moulded each into an earplug and pressed them into Starlight's ears.

'Now we can wake him,' Sir Chadwick said.

It was harder than Abby expected. No matter how much they shook him, Starlight remained asleep.

They paused for a moment at a gentle squawk from Benbow.

'Do you want to try?' Abby asked him, and Benbow nodded.

They stood back and Benbow hopped on to Starlight's chest and began a little dance.

Captain Starlight began to stir. 'All right, Benbow,' he mumbled. 'I'll get your fish cakes.'

'Help him to his feet, quickly,' Sir Chadwick said. 'Keep low and hold his hands by his sides.'

When the captain stood swaying before them, Sir Chadwick took the ring from his pocket and ran around him several times. 'I'm binding his hands to his sides with the fairy thread,' he said breathlessly. 'There, that should do it.' With a last flourish he slipped the ring on Starlight's finger.

Abby had been so busy helping she hadn't noticed that the lane leading to Bright Town was now filled with people. They began calling Starlight's name.

'That's exactly what he mustn't hear,' Sir Chadwick said.

Abby looked at Starlight and now noticed that there was

a scroll sticking out of his pocket.

'Is that the second document?' she asked.

Sir Chadwick grabbed it. 'Yes, I do believe it is,' he said triumphantly. 'The Night Witches knew if Captain Starlight took it into Bright Town it would have been lost to us for ever.'

Before Sir Chadwick could unroll the missing scroll, Abby heard a terrible howling sound and the ground began to tremble. The scene around them dissolved. The gentle countryside of Bright Town vanished and they found themselves standing on the edge of a great ragged cliff that stood before a sea of molten fire. The sky was filled with dark clouds and torn by crashing lightning. A smell so foul came to Abby that she had to hold her nose.

A flock of bats came whirling and spiralling towards them. Abby screamed as the bats merged into one and formed the terrible figure the Night Witches called the Great One.

The Great Mandini
Answers the Call

'So, Chadwick,' the dreadful figure hissed. 'You have decided to meddle in my affairs again.'

Sir Chadwick had drawn his wand as if it were a sword. He reached out and pulled Abby back. She had to peep around him to see what was happening.

'Stand aside, Snivel,' Sir Chadwick said evenly.

'My name is Carstairs Wolfbane, you tin-pot Thespian,' the Chief of Night Witches snarled. 'You may call me *Great One*.'

Sir Chadwick smiled. 'It was Snivel Cheeseman when we were tutored by old Professor Calibar at Merlin College.'

'I changed it,' the Great One howled. 'Just as I changed old Calibar. I turned him into a spider, you know.'

'Well, you'll always be Snivel Cheeseman to me,' said Sir Chadwick lightly. 'The worst undergraduate that ever cheated in his examinations.'

'I want that document,' the Great One said. 'Give it to me and you can be on your way.'

'Sorry, Snivel, this is stolen property.'

Wolfbane also flourished his wand. 'I can cut through your fairy threads with this,' he threatened. 'See how you enjoy eternity here in the Lost Land.'

Sir Chadwick held up his own wand. 'Aloric the great wand-maker forged this for me. It is fully charged with Ice Dust. Enough to spike you like a red-hot poker passing through a snowman.'

'Then we have an impasse,' the Great One snarled.

'In that case,' Sir Chadwick replied, sweeping Abby into his arms, 'we'll be on our way. Think of those who love you, Abby, and pull on your thread,' he shouted.

Abby did as he instructed and as she felt the fairy thread begin to tighten, the Great One howled with rage and pointed his wand at Sir Chadwick. Purple light flashed from it and the document burst into flames just as Abby felt the familiar rushing sensation.

She entered the tunnel again. A few moments later there was the popping sound and she found herself back in Paint Lane.

The clock that had begun to strike as they left was still sounding. No time had passed. Sir Chadwick stood next to her, stamping on the blazing document as Captain Starlight and Benbow watched.

When the flames were extinguished he picked it up and stuffed it into his pocket. 'Back to the theatre,' he said and rapped on the door of number forty-six.

The cabbie opened the door and looked out suspiciously. 'What do you lot want now?' he demanded.

'Return us to Shaftesbury Avenue, my good man, and I will give you this,' Sir Chadwick said, producing a fifty-pound note from the pocket of his money suit. The taxi driver did not hesitate. He called over his shoulder. 'Put my dinner back in the oven, ma,' and slammed the door behind him.

Settled in the back of the cab, Sir Chadwick produced the charred document and carefully unrolled the remains. He studied it for a time, then said, 'The last part of the saga is destroyed but there's still a map.' He passed it to Captain Starlight. 'Can you read this?' he asked.

Starlight made his own examination, nodding his head thoughtfully. 'I can get us there,' he answered.

'Then the game is still afoot,' Sir Chadwick said as the cab drew up outside the Alhambra Theatre.

'That didn't take you long,' Spike said when Abby, Sir Chadwick, Benbow and Captain Starlight stood once more in Sir Chadwick's sitting room.

'We must have a council of war and make our plans,' Captain Starlight said, pulling the last of Sir Chadwick's stage-wax nose from his ears.

'Quite right,' Sir Chadwick agreed. 'The Night Witches know we are coming now. I fear we have lost the element of surprise.'

There was a gentle cough from Hilda. They turned to look at her.

'May I make a suggestion?' she said.

'By all means,' Sir Chadwick replied.

'Perhaps we need the services of the Great Mandini,' Hilda suggested.

Sir Chadwick frowned. 'Hmmm, the Great Mandini. He might be just the fellow to come up with a plan. Do you know where he can be found?'

'I can send a bird for him, Master.'

'Be so kind as to do that immediately.' He hesitated. 'And in view of our new relationship, you'd better call me Chadwick.'

Blushing, Hilda went to the window and a sparrow came and perched on her outstretched hand. She chirruped to the little bird and it shook its wings and flew off.

'Who is the Great Mandini?' Spike and Abby asked together.

'Brilliant fellow,' said Sir Chadwick. 'A master illusionist,

conjurer, and a great spell-maker. At least, he was until the
supplies of Ice Dust ran out.'

'If he can make spells, why does he bother with conjuring tricks?' Spike asked.

'That's just the point, lad,' Sir Chadwick replied with a
knowing smile. 'Any fool of a witch can make spells with
Ice Dust. A conjurer's tricks are far, far harder to perfect,
and the Great Mandini's are the very best.' He turned to
Hilda. 'Do you think it will take long?' As he spoke there
was a sudden peal of invisible trumpets, followed by a flash
of lightning.

Benbow gave a squawk, and when Spike and Abby's eyes
recovered from the dazzle, they saw a vast fat man dressed
in white tie and tails standing in the centre of the room
with a dove perched on each of his shoulders. 'You called,
Master?' he drawled, then he pointed to the doves which
immediately flew into the air and vanished.

Abby's gaze followed the doves. When she looked back,
the figure was now taller and very slim. He winked at Abby
and stroked his pencil-thin moustache.

'Mandini,' said Sir Chadwick. 'Good of you to come so
quickly.'

'As ever, Master, I am yours to command.'

'We need your advice.'

'What is the problem?'

'We have to invade the Night Witches' southern headquarters and they are expecting us.'

'How big are your forces?'

Sir Chadwick looked around the room. 'Just us. Captain Starlight, Benbow, Hilda Bluebell, Spike and Abby.'

'I admire your courage,' Mandini said with a slight bow.

Sir Chadwick nodded. 'Courage is not our problem. What we need is a plan.'

The Great Mandini stroked his moustache again. 'Simple,' he exclaimed. 'Create a diversion.' He pointed towards the door and everyone's eyes followed his finger.

When they looked back, only a fraction of a second later, he had changed into a kangaroo. Spike and Abby gasped. Then the kangaroo reached into its pouch and threw a handful of coloured handkerchiefs into the air. Abby's eyes followed the handkerchiefs. When she looked back, the kangaroo had vanished and the elegantly thin Mandini had returned.

'That's what you must do,' he said.

Sir Chadwick frowned. 'Turn into kangaroos?'

'No,' said the Great Mandini, with the hint of a sigh. 'Make the Night Witches look elsewhere.' Seeing their puzzled expressions, he added, 'Do you possess anything that will come as a surprise to them?'

They all thought and Captain Starlight said, 'Only the Atlantis Boat.'

Mandini raised his eyebrows. 'You actually have one?'

Starlight nodded. 'You've heard of them?'

'Only as legend. Are they as wondrous as the stories say?'

'Even better,' said Captain Starlight.

'There you are then.' Mandini walked to the table and picked up a bowl of flowers. 'This is the Night Witches' southern headquarters.'

They nodded.

'You must draw them out.' The flowers flew about the room. 'Then you can invade in their absence.'

'How?' asked Sir Chadwick.

'What do Night Witches like doing most?' said Mandini.

'Sinking the boats of Sea Witches,' growled Captain Starlight.

'Then it's easy,' replied the Great Mandini. 'The Sea Witch fleet must take to the seas and lure out the Night Witch Shark Boat fleet. That will give you your diversion and you can invade their headquarters.'

'But if we fail, they will destroy the entire Sea Witch fleet,' said Starlight.

'Nothing ventured, nothing gained,' said Mandini easily.

'He's right,' said Sir Chadwick. 'If we don't attack they will atomize us all anyway. It's victory or nothing.'

'I should be honoured to accompany you on this mission, Master,' said the Great Mandini.

Sir Chadwick clapped him on the shoulder. 'Good man, your services may prove to be invaluable.' Then he paused. 'But I am not commanding this venture.' He looked towards Captain Starlight. 'You are the senior naval man present, Captain. You must lead us.'

Starlight nodded. 'So be it. But first we must journey to Speller to put the plan to the Sea Witches.'

'We're going home?' said Abby.

'A spot of leave before the battle,' said Sir Chadwick.

'Perhaps I'll have time for a swim,' said Spike.

Good News
for the Citizens
of Speller

The Thames lapped over the Atlantis Boat as they sank below Embankment pier and forged downstream underwater. There was room for everyone in the cabin, although Mandini and Sir Chadwick crowded around the control panel while Captain Starlight explained the workings of the boat.

'What beautiful workmanship,' Mandini exclaimed. 'More art than craft. And you say the engines work on salt?'

Starlight nodded. 'Extracted from the sea water.'

'What elegance, what style.'

'She's tough as well,' Starlight said proudly. 'I reckon I could ram her straight through the hull of a Shark Boat.'

'Well, only as a last resort, I hope,' said Sir Chadwick.

Meanwhile, Spike and Abby sat with Hilda, who was teaching them a few notes of birdspeak. Abby found she was best at blackbirds and thrushes, but Spike was awfully good at owls and pigeons. Benbow had settled down in a seat on his own.

'We're well into the Thames estuary now,' Captain Starlight announced after taking a sighting through the crystal ball. 'Take your seats and buckle your seat belts. I'm heading for Speller at top speed.'

Starlight pushed on the throttle and Abby could feel the boat surge forward.

'Wonderful, wonderful!' Mandini exclaimed, but Sir Chadwick remained thoughtful and silent.

'Is everything all right?' Abby asked him.

He nodded with a faint smile. 'Just takes me a little time to get my sea-legs.'

'There's no waves down here, Sir Chadwick.' Spike said. 'You can't be seasick underwater.'

'I think it may be more of a mental condition,' said Sir Chadwick. 'I used to feel quite ill when my nanny took me boating on the Serpentine.'

'Try one of these,' said Captain Starlight, handing him a small paper bag. 'They're Boston peppermints.'

Sir Chadwick took one and popped it into his mouth with a doubtful expression. After a moment, he smiled broadly and nodded. 'Capital, capital. I feel better already, Captain.'

'They never fail,' replied Starlight, looking into the crystal ball again.

'Speller cove on the starboard bow already,' he called

out. 'We'll be docking in the harbour in a moment.' The
Atlantis Boat slowed down and Captain Starlight brought
her to the surface.

It was late evening in Speller and the reflection from
the lights of the town danced and twinkled in the dark,
lapping waters of the harbour. From the Town Hall came
the sound of the band. Abby could distinguish the sound of
Uncle Ben's French horn quite clearly and felt suddenly
very happy to be home. Having been away, even for such a
short time, made her realise how much she loved the little
town.

She wanted to rush ahead to see her aunt and uncle but
was torn by wanting to hear what Sir Chadwick, Starlight
and Mandini were saying.

'What a charming resort,' said Mandini, looking about
him with admiration at the neat rows of whitewashed cot-
tages. 'I had no idea it would be so delightful.'

'Nearly as pretty as Bright Town used to be,' said
Starlight gruffly.

'Have you heard of it, Mr Mandini?' Abby asked.

'Oh, yes, my dear,' he replied. 'All Light Witches have
heard of Speller. But I imagined it would be some sort of
dreary industrial port.'

Sir Chadwick laughed. 'We had to put that thought in
the minds of all the Light Witches. You know what an
impatient lot they are. They would all have been coming
down here to collect their supplies of Ice Dust straight
from the boats. Next thing you know, they would have

been taking their holidays here and squabbling with the townspeople.'

'It's a great privilege to visit, Chadwick,' said Hilda. He smiled and squeezed her hand awkwardly.

'Why is that music playing, child?' Sir Chadwick asked Abby

'It's the weekly dance,' she explained. 'All the citizens will be in the Town Hall.'

'Excellent,' Sir Chadwick said. 'Lead on, Abby. We can address everyone at the same time.'

Abby took them to the Town Hall and led the party into the assembly room where the dance was in full swing. As they entered, Uncle Ben was making an announcement. 'Take your partners for *The Sea Witch Horn Pipe.*' The band struck up and all the people of Speller linked arms and began to parade around the dance floor. At certain intervals, they did an intricate little jig on the spot.

While the townsfolk continued to dance, Abby and her party waited at the back of the hall until the music ended. Then Aunt Lucy saw Abby and Spike and rushed forward to embrace them. It was clear from her relief that she had been worried about them.

'Look, Ben, the children,' she called out happily to her husband, who immediately jumped down from the stage to hug them as well.

Abby introduced Sir Chadwick, Hilda, and the Great Mandini.

'Perhaps we could all go up on to the stage,' said Sir

Chadwick. 'I have an announcement to make.' He stood facing the crowd, who looked puzzled by the sudden arrival of outsiders. 'Citizens of Speller, I'm sorry to interrupt the dance,' said Sir Chadwick, 'but I have urgent need to address you all. Some of you may remember me. I am Sir Chadwick Street, Master of the Light Witches.'

'We remember you, Sir Chadwick,' someone called out. 'But what brings you here now? The Witch Trade is finished.'

Sir Chadwick held up his hands. 'I have important news for you. I am here, with my companions, on a special mission of vital importance to us all.' He paused and gestured to the others of his party. 'Many of you may remember me but allow me to introduce my friends. Abby and Spike you all know. This is Captain Adam Starlight, also called by some the Ancient Mariner.'

There was a murmur of surprise from the crowd at the mention of such a famous figure. Sir Chadwick pointed to the rafters of the hall. 'Up there is his feathered friend, Benbow. Next is my assistant Hilda Bluebell, and last but certainly not least, the Great Mandini, master of magic and illusion.' Mandini bowed at his introduction and allowed a dove to flutter from his sleeve.

'How can we help you, Master? Mr Halyard called from the dance floor.

'I have good news and I have grave news,' Sir Chadwick continued. 'First, the good news. We believe the lost children of Speller may still be alive, held captive as slaves by the Night Witches.'

'Alive! Our children may be alive,' the words flowed around the hall in an outburst of joy and disbelief. Sir Chadwick held up his hand for silence, but it was some minutes before calm was sufficiently restored for them to hear what else he had to say.

'Yes, *alive*, but in danger. We all know the Night Witches have driven you from the oceans with their fleet of Shark Boats. You all thought you would be safe as long as you didn't put to sea again but stayed here, protected by the very walls of Speller.

'I am here to tell you that time is over! The Night Witches have devised a terrible machine that can destroy us all. Even now, they are plotting to attack.'

There was more uproar in the room and Sir Chadwick held up his hands for silence. Gradually, the noise died down.

'What can we do?' Mr Halyard asked.

Sir Chadwick held his wand aloft like a sword. 'Attack is the best form of defence. My companions and I are prepared to invade their headquarters, free their prisoners and seize the Ice Dust they have stockpiled. But we need your help in this dangerous venture.'

'What do you want us to do?' called out Mr Halyard.

'We need a diversion,' explained Sir Chadwick. 'Something that will tempt the Shark Boat fleet out of their home port so that we can penetrate their defences.' He paused dramatically. 'What I am asking you to do will need every

ounce of your courage... We want you to take the Sea
Witch fleet to sea.'

The uproar in the hall was deafening as the Sea Witches
heatedly discussed the possible outcomes of Sir Chadwick's
proposal. Finally, Mr Halyard put up his hand once more.
'We don't lack the courage for a fight, Master. But we are
defenceless against the Shark Boats. They will sink us all.'

'You have cannon, don't you?' Captain Starlight
called out.

'We do, but our cannonballs are useless against their
armour.'

'What if you had cannon balls made of Ice Dust?'

'Impossible,' replied Mr Halyard. 'You must know we
don't have a pinch of Ice Dust left in Speller. If we did, it
would be a different matter.'

'What if we can get you all you need?'

'Then we'd send them all to the bottom of the sea.'

'Well, this is our plan,' Sir Chadwick continued. 'We
shall set out for their headquarters. You will put out to
sea. The Night Witches will know you are coming and
they will set out to attack you. When they sail we shall
invade their headquarters, free their prisoners, take their
supplies of Ice Dust and meet with you on the high seas.
There will be enough Ice Dust to arm the Sea Witch fleet
and win a battle against the Shark Boats.'

Mr Halyard spoke again. 'You'll have to move pretty
fast to manage that.'

'We can do it,' Sir Chadwick replied confidently. 'I'm

not saying there won't be casualties. But Hilda Bluebell will sail with you. She is a Light Witch and trained in the arts of healing, should any of you be injured in the fight.'

Mr Halyard looked around at the townsfolk. 'It looks as if we're going to sea again, lads and lasses,' he said. There was a momentary pause and then a great, swelling cheer rose up from the Sea Witches.

After the meeting in the Town Hall, Aunt Lucy had asked Abby and her friends to come back for supper. When the meal was finished they all sat around the long wooden table in the kitchen.

Sir Chadwick sighed with contentment. 'I had quite forgotten what a magnificent dish Speller sausage surprise could be,' he said. 'You must give me the recipe. My man, Shuffle, can prepare it for me back in London.'

'It's the herbs and spices,' said Lucy, pleased by the compliment.

'Another mug of beer, Sir Chadwick?' offered Ben.

'Just one more then we must go to our bunks,' said Captain Starlight. 'We sail on the morning tide.'

'Well, you children can go up after one more hand of cards,' said Aunt Lucy noticing they had been playing snap with Hilda. 'And I'm sure Hilda won't want any beer. When you're ready I'll show you to your bed, my dear.'

She turned to Abby and Spike and put her arms about them. 'Look after them tomorrow, gentlemen. They are very young to go on such an adventure.'

'We shall guard them with our lives, Ma'am,' Captain Starlight replied.

'Rely on us,' added Mandini.

'On my word of honour,' said Sir Chadwick.

'Thank you, gentlemen,' Lucy said, just managing to hold back her tears.

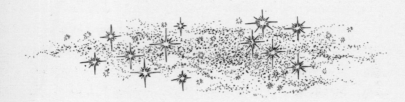

The Sea Witch Fleet Sails Again

The first light of dawn was turning the colour of the sea from grey to dark green when Captain Starlight assembled his crew in Lucy and Ben's kitchen. Abby, Spike, the Great Mandini and Sir Chadwick stood in a row while he inspected them. 'Now, you've all got Atlantis coats,' he said in a gruff voice. 'In addition, I want you to draw a jack-knife and a length of twine from the stores.'

He stopped and clasped his hands behind his back. 'Just a word about discipline before we set out. There can only be one captain on a boat. You must obey his word without question. Your life or the life of another member of the crew may depend upon it. So if I give an order, don't ask, "Why?" Just do it. Understand?'

'Yes, Captain,' they all replied.

Starlight smiled. 'And another thing, at sea we say *aye aye*, not *yes*.'

'Aye aye, Captain,' they replied smartly.

'Now, for our first duty.' He took a large watch from his pocket. 'In half an hour, the townsfolk will be aboard the Sea Witch fleet in the cavern. We shall be out in the cove on the Atlantis Boat. I will open the cliff face and the Sea Witch fleet will set sail.

'I think it would be best for us to have another Light Witch with the Sea Witch fleet, so the Great Mandini will transfer to the fastest sailing ship once we see which vessel has the best turn of speed. Any questions?'

The crew silently shook their heads.

'Good. Well, let's get aboard.'

As they left the shop, they found the whole population of Speller waiting in silence for them in the lane outside. At their appearance, the Sea Witches gave a great cheer. Lucy, Ben and Hilda, along with all of the townsfolk, accompanied them to the harbour.

Aunt Lucy and Uncle Ben hugged Abby and Spike goodbye, and Hilda suddenly threw her arms around Sir Chadwick's neck and kissed him.

'Come back to me,' she said. Sir Chadwick removed his battered tweed hat with a flourish. 'If it takes all eternity, my love,' he replied, and Lucy wiped a tear from her cheek at the romance of it all.

Captain Starlight called out, 'Sea Witches to your ships, I will open the cliff entrance in exactly half an hour.'

Captain Starlight sailed from the harbour and after a few minutes' cruising they reached the cove. He throttled back so that the Atlantis Boat bobbed gently on the swell of the morning tide. It was a bright day and the sun bathed the cove in a golden light.

After consulting his watch, Captain Starlight blew a long blast on the horn of the Atlantis Boat. Abby and Spike watched the great cliff open and as the sails caught the morning wind, the fleet of the Sea Witches came out into the open sea. Abby had never seen such a wonderful sight.

'Magnificent!' exclaimed Sir Chadwick. 'What a noble moment.' The wind filled the sails of the vast armada as the ships fanned out into the bay. A three-masted schooner quickly pulled ahead and Abby called out, 'It's Mr Halyard's ship – and Hilda is on board her.'

Starlight said, 'There's your flag ship, Mandini. Prepare to transfer.'

'Aye aye,' replied Mandini.

Starlight brought the Atlantis Boat alongside the schooner as it tacked against the wind.

'Fine seamanship,' Starlight said. 'Those captains know their business right enough.'

The schooner was now close to the Atlantis Boat. Abby and Spike waved to Mr Halyard at the helm.

'To think that all the time we've known the townsfolk, we hadn't realised what wonderful sailors they are,' Abby said to Spike.

'Yes,' replied Spike. 'I thought they just liked dressing up as if they went to sea.'

'Appearances can be deceptive,' said Mandini, suddenly plucking a fresh herring from behind Spike's left ear. He threw it into the air where it turned into a seagull and soared away.

'Throw me a line, if you please Captain,' Mandini called out to Mr Halyard. The rope snaked down on to the deck of the Atlantis Boat. Mandini seized it with one hand and seemed to float up to the deck of the schooner.

'Good luck,' Starlight called out to Mandini, who now stood next to Mr Halyard. 'We'll see you soon.'

'How will they know where to meet us?' Spike asked.

'Benbow will take them a message,' Starlight answered. Then he turned to his crew. 'Time to go below.'

Abby and Spike waved once more at the fleet of ships racing before the wind and Sir Chadwick exchanged a final salute with Hilda, who stood in the prow of the schooner. Then they followed Starlight down into the cabin. Sir Chadwick closed the hatch and the Atlantis Boat dived beneath the waves.

Captain Starlight Takes his Revenge

'What's the fastest she'll go underwater, Captain?' Sir Chadwick asked when they had settled themselves in the cabin.

'I don't really know,' Starlight replied, not taking his eyes off the controls. 'I've never had one up to full speed. She does better than a thousand leagues an hour when she's flying.'

'She flies as well!'

Starlight nodded. 'The Night Witches have systems to warn them of anything coming by land or sky. But they don't have anything that works under the sea. So we can stick between the mountain ranges on the seabed.'

Starlight made some adjustments to the controls to set the boat on an automatic course. Then he came and sat next to the rest of the crew at the chart table. Taking the fragment of map that Sir Chadwick had managed to save, he held it up. After a few moments they could see that a small image of the fragment had appeared inside the crystal ball.

'The crystal has a store of maps of the world throughout history,' he explained. 'It will match this to the chart from which it was originally copied.' As they all looked into the crystal, the map dissolved and another version took its place. 'This is interesting,' Starlight said.

'What is?' asked Sir Chadwick.

'The original map was of an island off the coast of Antarctica. This is a later version showing that the ice of Antarctica has covered it. The original island is part of Antarctica now.'

'I thought the Atlantis Boat was thousands of years old,' Spike said. 'How has it got a modern map showing how the world is now?'

Starlight shrugged. 'Don't ask me, lad,' he replied. 'There's a lot about this boat I don't understand. Sometimes it seems to have a mind of its own. All I'm saying is that the original island isn't the same any more.'

'I wonder what happened,' Sir Chadwick said.

'There was a soft squawking from Benbow.

'What did you say?' Captain Starlight asked.

Benbow squawked again.

'You're right, Benbow,' Starlight said.

'What did he say, Captain?' asked Abby.

'Ask the whales. The whales know everything about the seas and they pass on the information from generation to generation. We'd better keep an eye out until we can ask one of them what happened.'

'But do we know where we're going now?' asked Spike.

'Well, the Atlantis Boat certainly seems to,' Starlight said. 'Wait a minute. Just look at this.'

Another picture had appeared in the crystal. It showed a bay filled with Shark Boats. The whole landscape of ice and snow looked bleak and uninviting. The sea was almost as black as the ships that floated at their moorings.

'It doesn't look very nice,' Abby said quietly.

'No, it isn't,' said Spike.

'I'd forgotten that you've been there, Spike,' she said. 'Do you remember this place?'

Spike shook his head.

Starlight continued to look into the crystal. They could now see Night Witches swarming over the boats.

Sir Chadwick had been sitting thoughtfully but now he spoke. 'Would you all be quiet for a moment? I'm going to try an experiment.'

They all watched in silence as Sir Chadwick hunched in his chair with a frown on his forehead. Then, after a few minutes, he sat up and pointed at the crystal ball. The image of the bay faded and they could see an empty theatre that was open to the sky.

A very young man in doublet and hose, with a cape over one shoulder, walked on to the stage and stood nervously in the light from burning torches.

'Are you ready, lad?' a voice asked.

The young man nodded and Abby recognised him. 'Look, Spike, that's Sir Chadwick when he was very young.'

'What are you going to do for us?' the voice asked.

'The prologue from your play, *Henry V*, Sir.'

'There's no need to call me sir, lad. I'm just an actor like yourself. When you're ready.'

The young Sir Chadwick struck an extravagant pose but before he spoke the image faded from the crystal ball. 'That's enough of that,' Sir Chadwick said.

'Who were you speaking to?' asked Spike.

'Actually, it was Will Shakespeare himself,' said Sir Chadwick diffidently. 'That was my first audition, at the Globe theatre.'

'How did you manage to make that appear?' Starlight asked.

'I was experimenting with the boat.' Sir Chadwick said. 'And my experiment worked.'

'What gave you the idea?' Abby asked.

Sir Chadwick pointed to Starlight. 'It was something the captain said.'

'What did I say?'

'Your words were, "Sometimes it was as if the boat had a mind of its own." Well, it does. When Spike asked if we knew where we were going the boat showed us our destination.'

'Are you saying the boat can think?' Starlight said dubiously.

'Possibly,' Sir Chadwick replied. 'It can certainly read minds. Mentally, I just asked it to recall that moment from my past and you saw that it could capture my memories and show them in the crystal ball.'

'How can we be sure it can think?' asked Starlight.

'Why don't we ask it?' suggested Abby.

'Go on then,' Starlight urged. 'Give it a try.'

Abby looked at the crystal ball. 'Boat, can you think?' she asked.

There was a chime of musical notes and a melodious woman's voice answered, 'Yes, Abby.'

They all exchanged glances.

'Are you alive?' Abby continued.

Now there was a chuckle. 'Not in the way you are.'

'What are you, then?'

'I am a machine that learns.'

'So you're not human?' Sir Chadwick asked.

The laughter came again. 'No.'

'What makes you work?' Spike said.

'Kindness.'

'Can you explain that?' Starlight asked.

'Ask Abby.'

They looked towards her.

'Do you understand?' Sir Chadwick asked.

Abby thought. 'I'm not sure, but my Aunt Lucy always says a crust given in kindness is worth more than a careless feast from a prince.'

Sir Chadwick leaned forward. 'Are you saying kind people make you work?'

'Something like that. Kind people who want to perform good deeds. I am not for pleasure alone.'

'How clever are you?' Spike asked.

'As clever as you want me to be.'

'Why didn't you speak before?' Starlight said.

'You never asked me.'

'I think I'm beginning to understand,' said Sir Chadwick. 'You can only help us if we want to perform kind deeds.'

'Yes.'

'What if we're bad?'

'Then I would be of no use to you at all.'

'So the Night Witches couldn't make use of you?'

'No.'

'Can you tell us what to do?'

'I cannot. Those who made me did not want me to be superior to human beings. I can only help when you ask — and if your heart is true.'

Sir Chadwick smiled. *'My strength is as the strength of ten because my heart is pure.'*

'What's that?' asked Spike.

'It's from *Sir Galahad* by Alfred Lord Tennyson, a great story about a valiant knight, told in verse.'

'Now you understand,' said the boat's voice. There was a pause and it spoke again. 'Mountain range ahead. Please be seated and fasten safety belts.'

The boat began to rise and fall like a giant rollercoaster. They all sat enthralled, watching on the screen the mountains and valleys of the seabed they were skimming above.

After a time, Captain Starlight, who was sitting at the control panel, looked around at the rest of the crew. Abby and Spike appeared to be enjoying the ride, but the rest of the party were looking a little queasy.

'It's getting dark now,' Starlight said. 'I think I'll risk taking her up to the surface for a time, it will less bumpy.'

'As you wish, Captain,' Sir Chadwick said, and Abby thought he looked a little relieved.

When they were close to the surface, Starlight glanced at the crystal ball. 'Icebergs ahead,' he said.

'Are we likely to collide with one?' Abby asked.

Starlight shook his head. 'No, but we might begin to zigzag at an uncomfortable speed. I think I'll slow down. Why don't you all take a rest?'

'What about you, Captain?' Abby asked. Starlight chuckled. 'I'm so old, child, I don't need much sleep.'

'Well, I'm even older,' said Sir Chadwick. 'But I could manage forty winks.'

Some time later, Abby woke to find Starlight gently shaking her shoulder. 'I thought you'd want to know, there's a Shark Boat submarine ahead of us,' he said. 'We're going to slip past it.'

Abby looked at the crystal ball. She could see a sinister black shape hovering in the water ahead.

'Now what are they up to?' Abby asked.

'Some mischief, I'll be bound,' Starlight said. 'I'll scan the surrounding area.'

'What's happening, Captain?' Sir Chadwick asked as he also woke from a gentle doze.

'Shark Boat submarine,' Starlight replied, studying the crystal again. 'It's hiding beneath an iceberg.'

Abby watched it in the crystal ball. 'Do you think

they're looking for us?' she asked.

Before Starlight could answer, they heard the sound of whistling and clicking.

'A whale is coming,' Starlight answered. 'I think the Shark Boat is waiting to harpoon her.'

'Why do you think that?' Abby said.

Starlight nodded to the crystal ball. 'Night Witches eat whales.'

As he spoke, the submarine began to rise to the surface, close to the side of the iceberg that would conceal it from the approaching whale.

'Ah,' said Starlight. 'It's going to hide on the far side of the iceberg. When the whale passes they'll harpoon her.'

'Can't we warn the whale?' Abby said.

'We can do better than that,' Starlight said grimly and he opened a locker and took out his harpoon. The blade looked old and dull as he wiped it with his leathery hand. 'May I trouble you for a touch of Ice Dust, Sir Chadwick,' Starlight said.

'Certainly,' Sir Chadwick replied, producing his wand.

'Just a sprinkle on the blade,' Starlight said grimly.

Sir Chadwick followed his instruction and the dull metal suddenly glowed with a bluish light. Then the whole blade shone as though it were made of beaten silver.

'We're going up,' Starlight said, and the Atlantis Boat began to rise to the surface.

'Take the controls, Sir Chadwick,' he said, 'and bring us alongside the whale.'

'I'll do my best,' Sir Chadwick replied, seizing the wheel. 'Oh, I say,' he exclaimed,' she handles beautifully. Like an old sports car I used to have.'

They came to the surface and Starlight slid back the hatch so that they were exposed to the night air. Abby could see everything quite clearly by the light of a bright moon, which reflected on the glittering sea. The gigantic iceberg glowed in the light, and to their left she could see the whale coursing through the calm ocean.

Starlight began to call out in the whistling and clicking language. The whale seemed unconcerned by their sudden arrival but it nodded its massive head in acknowledgement of Starlight's warning.

They were so close to her now, Abby could see one of her great eyes gazing at them. Spike, who could also understand the language, translated for Abby. 'He's warned her of the Shark Boat.'

'Take her dead ahead, Sir Chadwick, if you please,' Starlight called out.

'Where is the Shark Boat now?' asked Abby.

'Hidden on the far side of the iceberg,' Starlight replied. 'Keep her steady.' Sir Chadwick brought the boat to the dark side of the iceberg and, just as Abby thought they must collide, Starlight suddenly shouted, 'Light!'

At his command, a bright blue beam coming from the prow of the Atlantis Boat illuminated the shadowy side of the iceberg. In the sudden glare, Abby could see two Night Witches standing at the prow of the submarine. They were holding harpoons at the ready. They looked up and cowered in shocked surprise, caught in the sudden dazzling light.

'Steer close to their starboard side,' Starlight ordered and, as they came almost within touching distance of the submarine, he roared out, *'Remember Bright Town!'* and threw his great harpoon at the side of the Shark Boat.

'Hang on!' Starlight warned his crew. 'Full ahead, hard to port.'

Sir Chadwick steered the boat to the left and they all looked back. They saw the flash of an explosion. There was a silence, and then a mighty booming bang, like a great gun firing, rolled across the sea.

'Stop,' Starlight ordered and the Atlantis Boat came to a

halt, bobbing on the surface of the sea.

Spike and Abby wrinkled their noses as a dreadful smell, like old dustbins, wafted across the water. Starlight was pulling on the rope attached to his harpoon and finally hauled it back aboard.

The whale the Shark Boat had been hunting came alongside them, and gently nudged the Atlantis Boat. Starlight reached out and slapped her great grey flank. Then he spoke a greeting in the special language before he turned to Spike.

He said, 'Here lad, you talk to her, I'm a bit rusty in whale language.'

Spike leaned over the side of the Atlantis Boat and began to speak to the great creature.

'Ask her about the island,' Starlight said.

Spike continued talking for a time, then he turned to the others.

'She says that long ago, when all the world's ships had sails, the sea around the island grew cold because the fires inside the dome became feeble. Eventually the island froze to the mainland.'

'So the volcanoes became extinct,' Starlight said. 'And did the underground river freeze up?'

Spike asked the question and the whale replied.

'No. But she says the terrible creature still lives in the river. The great monster that eats all living things.'

Abby remembered the saga. 'So it's still alive?'

'The whale says the creature never dies.'

'Does it fear anything?'

Spike asked the question and looked surprised by the whale's answer. He turned to the others and said. 'The monster fears kindness. At least I think she said "fears".'

They all looked at each other.

'A strange coincidence that the same word "kindness" should come up so soon,' Sir Chadwick said, and then added, 'or maybe not.'

'Best be on our way now,' Starlight said. 'Thank her for us all, lad.'

Spike did what Starlight asked and with a clicking whistle of farewell, the whale slid beneath the waves.

Captain Starlight took over the controls again and sealed the cabin so they could submerge. 'I'm going to put her on full power and use the automatic pilot,' he said. 'So take your seats.'

The Atlantis Boat hurtled forward and Abby could see the bed of the ocean on the display screen as they surged forwards.

The boat twisted and turned, rose and fell to follow the contours of the strange landscape beneath the sea. It was like some never-ending magical fairground ride.

'Let's all get some more rest,' Starlight suggested. 'The boat will warn us if there is any danger.'

They all lay back in their chairs and closed their eyes while the Atlantis Boat hurtled on towards its destination.

Inside the Great
Dome of Ice

*A*bby and Spike woke up again as Captain Starlight began to ease back the speed of the Atlantis Boat and started to surface. A moment later, Sir Chadwick blinked his eyes open. 'We're coming to the edge of Antarctica,' Starlight announced. 'Let's go on deck and take a look.'

Abby felt quite warm in her Atlantis cape, but the icy air chilled her face when they stood on deck. For a few moments they all stood in silence, overcome by the scene that greeted them. The sea and sky were velvet black, but light from the millions of shining stars above reflected from the ice and snow that stretched before them.

'According to my calculations,' said Starlight, 'the mouth of the river should be quite close.' As he spoke there was a sudden glow of intensely bright light some miles away along the coastline.

'What do you think that can be?' Sir Chadwick asked.

Starlight took an instrument that looked like a short

telescope and aimed it towards the source of the light. After studying it for a time, he handed the instrument to Abby. She peered through the eyepiece and could see a cove which must have lain over the horizon. It was the place they had seen in the crystal ball.

Harsh white floodlights lit the scene. Long concrete jetties stretched into the sea. Moored alongside were row after row of Shark Boats. Next to them were vast sledges that were discharging their cargoes into some of the open hatches of the Night Witch fleet. When the sledges were empty, they were reloaded with vast drums.

'That's the Night Witch port,' Starlight said, taking the viewing instrument from Abby and making some adjustments before raising it to his own eye.

'Yes!' he exclaimed. 'I can see a great tunnel leading into the cliffs. They must have cut their way in again, like Mordoc did. They still seem to be working on the entrance, they're making it much larger.' He turned to the others. 'Everyone below now. We must find the mouth of the river.'

Captain Starlight steered the Atlantis Boat along the coastline away from the port where the Shark Boats were unloading. As dawn was breaking, they were travelling at a fairly low speed when suddenly the prow of the Atlantis Boat swung away from the coast. A powerful current was pushing them further out to sea.

'That must be the river,' Spike said as Starlight brought the boat around and increased power to head against the flow. Abby, Spike, Starlight and Sir Chadwick watched in the crystal and after a few moments they could see the dark mouth of a tunnel that was easily wide enough for the Atlantis Boat to enter. 'There's no mist,' Starlight said. 'The river can't be as warm as it used to be.'

'Once more unto the breach, dear friends, once more,' Sir Chadwick murmured as they looked at the smooth surface of the icy tunnel that now surrounded them.

Captain Starlight warned them, 'Remember, one of the sailors in the Viking saga was eaten by the monster.'

As they passed through the tunnel, they could see nothing in the crystal ball except the smooth ice walls and occasional shoals of tiny darting fish.

'Light ahead,' said Starlight eventually. 'We're coming to the end of the tunnel.'

'According to the saga, the light inside the dome was red,' Spike said. They could all see that the glow from the end of the tunnel was white as snow. 'It must have changed when the volcanoes became extinct.'

'Let's go up and take a look,' Starlight answered as he steered the boat to the surface of the river. Abby, Spike, Starlight and Sir Chadwick gathered round the crystal ball to catch their first glimpse of the Land of Mordoc. The sight that greeted them was astonishing.

Four great orbs of light hung in the sky under the mighty dome and shone down to illuminate a landscape that was entirely white. Forests and mountains, fields and valleys – all they could see before them was frosted like a gigantic wedding cake. The river wound its way through the colourless vista like a great curling silver serpent. Abby could see the volcanoes that had once heated the land. Fine wisps of smoke curled from their brims but there was no sign of the raging fire they had heard about in the saga.

'The Night Witches must have made those artificial suns,' Sir Chadwick said.

'I can see their road now,' Abby exclaimed. They looked into the crystal ball and saw the highway that the Night Witches had cut from their tunnel. It led far away to the centre of the landscape. In the distance, they could see a mighty column of ice that rose to join the roof of the great dome above.

'That column is at least four or five miles wide,' Sir Chadwick said. 'What do you think, Captain?'

'Easily that,' replied Starlight. 'It must have once been

the wall of water described in the Viking saga. When the volcanoes became extinct it must have frozen into that great column.'

'I'm not sure they *are* completely extinct,' Sir Chadwick said. 'I don't think extinct volcanoes continue to smoke. Perhaps *dormant* might be a better word.'

'Does any of this look familiar to you, Spike?' Abby asked.

Spike shook his head. 'All I get are hazy bits. As it is when you try to recall a tune or a word that's on the tip of your tongue.'

'Well, that column of ice is where we must go eventually,' Captain Starlight said.

Later, while the Atlantis Boat continued to cruise beneath the surface of the river, Starlight called for a conference. 'We need more information,' he said. 'The crystal ball and the telescope are useful but we need greater detail now. Someone will have to scout ahead and tell us how the land lies.'

They gazed at each other... then everyone spoke at once: 'I'll go.'

Starlight shook his head. 'It wouldn't be practical. You'd have to go on foot, and that would take too long.'

'I could go with Benbow carrying me,' Abby volunteered. 'At least we would be invisible.'

Starlight nodded. 'I was thinking the same. But you're a brave girl to offer all the same.'

'We're coming closer to the road,' Spike called out from where he had been keeping an eye on the crystal ball.

Sure enough, the river, in its twisting course, had

brought them close to the Night Witches' highway. Starlight stopped the boat and they all gathered around the crystal ball. Now, they could see quite clearly how the Night Witches had hacked a great tunnel to enter the land enclosed in the dome. Their road was like a wide black slash across the landscape, and led to the mighty column of ice in the centre of the Land of Mordoc.

As they watched, a great sledge approached from the direction of the ice column. It was a crude affair, like a wagon, but with runners instead of wheels. Instead of horses, children were harnessed to haul the load. A Night Witch sat on the driver's seat, and two trolls walked alongside the children, cracking the long whips they carried.

Starlight started the engine and moved the boat further up-river. When they were far away from the road, he stopped again and turned to Abby. 'Do you still remember your tune?'

She nodded.

'Don't take too many risks. And when you are aloft, remember to memorise this location so you can find your way back to us.'

'Aye aye, Captain.'

'I've rigged up the harness, so you won't have to hold on to Benbow's feet all the time.' He handed her a pair of dark goggles. 'And you might find these useful if you go near those artificial suns.'

Abby hung them around her neck. She was beginning to feel slightly scared at the prospect of leaving the others.

Benbow seemed to read her mind. He nuzzled her with his great beak and somehow she felt better.

'Now I'm going to raise the hatch and let Benbow take you straight up from the cabin. Just in case that serpent is about,' said Starlight.

As the hatch drew back, cold air filled the cabin. Abby whistled her tune and disappeared. Benbow hovered above her as she reached up and clipped herself into the harness. As they soared aloft, the first thing Abby noticed was the silence. Benbow carried her higher and higher and, gradually, she could make out the features of the land below her.

It was very like the pictures she had seen in the elves' fire when Wooty had read the saga, but now everything was frosted white. The river coiled around mountains, crossed plains and passed through forests. Everything looked tranquil and quite beautiful, except where the ugly gash of the Night Witches' road cut across the land.

They were getting quite close to one of the artificial suns. 'Take me closer, Benbow,' Abby called out as she slipped the goggles over her eyes. The great bird climbed even higher but Abby felt no extra heat coming from the harsh, glaring light.

Suddenly, she became aware of a distinct humming sound, like a hive of angry bees.

They were now almost up to the ceiling of the dome. Abby could see it was quite smooth. The goggles dimmed the glare from the artificial suns enough for her to make out what was causing the sound.

To Abby's amazement, it looked like some great mechanical insect. The humming sound came from four huge sets of wings that were beating so fast they were no more than a blur in the cold air. The thing was studded all over with thousands of tiny bulbs of light. As they circled the contraption, she suddenly heard another sound above the hum of the artificial suns.

It was the throb of approaching engines. An airship was gliding towards them. Like all of the things made by the Night Witches, the gasbag looked sinister — like an enormous prehistoric monster.

Peering from beneath one of Benbow's wings, Abby could see a gondola hanging beneath the airship. She could also make out two crew members. Both wore black flying helmets, goggles and heavy overcoats. One operated the controls while the other examined the artificial suns.

Abby watched as the airship stopped above the great machine. The crewman who had been scanning the surface of the light was lowered on a harness. He carried a large shoulder bag. Abby was puzzled for a moment, until she realised he was changing the dead bulbs.

When the job was finished, the airship crewman signalled to the pilot, who winched him back on board.

Abby had seen enough. 'Take me to the column of ice now, please, Benbow,' she called and he wheeled about and headed for the distant horizon.

Distance was deceptive in the still, clear air. It was much, much further than Abby had estimated. They seemed to be flying for hours and Abby was glad of the harness Captain Starlight had rigged up. Her arms would have been very tired if she'd had to hold on to Benbow's legs all this time.

'It won't be long now, Benbow,' she called out simply to make a noise. She was tired of the unbroken silence.

At long last, there seemed to be only a few more miles to travel. But suddenly, they were plunged into deep darkness. It took Abby a moment to realise that the artificial suns had been switched off. She could no longer feel the gentle breeze on her face so she guessed that Benbow had stopped and was now hovering in midair. 'Of course,' Abby said aloud. 'The Night Witches don't like too much light. They must be giving themselves a rest in the dark. We'd better go down, Benbow.'

As they descended, her eyes gradually became used to the dimness. There was the faintest amount of light penetrating the thick ice and snow on the roof of the dome but not enough for them to continue their journey.

Slowly, Benbow descended into the forest below. They found a clearing beneath the frozen trees and came to rest on a bank of snow. Abby realised there was little she could do until the lights came on again, so she made the best of things.

'I think we might as well get some sleep, Benbow,' she said. 'There's room in my cloak for the two of us.'

So, with Benbow snuggling up to her, she lay down. Protected by her Atlantis cape from the cold of the deep snow, they were soon asleep.

Inside the Great Column of Ice

*A*bby woke up once while it was still dark. She thought she could hear the sound of someone crying quite close to where she and Benbow lay. But when she opened her eyes there was only silence. After a few moments she drifted off to sleep again.

All at once the artificial suns blazed into life.

Abby sat up and rubbed her eyes. She saw that the snowdrift on which they had slept was close to the mouth of a little cave. For a moment, she remembered she'd heard someone crying in the dark, but that was put out of her mind when she saw through the trees that the riverbank was just a few yards away.

Abby shuddered, thinking how near they had been to where the serpent lived. She considered exploring the cave but decided they had better continue their journey to the column of ice.

'Take us up, Benbow,' she called out when she had adjusted her harness.

Again, they soared into the air above the forest. As they approached their destination, Abby could see how massive the great column of ice truly was. The outside was rough and gnarled like the bark of an ancient oak tree, but where the column reached the roof, it seemed to dwindle to a mere thread in the sky.

At the base, Abby saw another great tunnel hacked into the gnarled wall of ice. There were guards on either side and gangs of trolls watched as ragged children, wrapped in rags against the cold, toiled to make it even wider.

'Take us inside, Benbow,' Abby called out, and he swooped down to enter the tunnel above the heads of the working children. Some looked up at the sound of Benbow's beating wings, but they saw nothing.

Abby could feel the air grow warmer as they flew along the passageway. They emerged in an entirely different landscape from the one they had just left.

Another great forest stretched before them, filled with trees that were all the colours of the rainbow. Fruit hung from vines and branches and brightly plumed birds flitted among the looping vines. The Night Witches' road still cut into the forest but, when Benbow soared above the trees, their branches concealed it.

Abby could see something else in the centre of the new landscape – a lake of crystal clear water the colour of sapphires and, overlooking it, a great castle made of silvery stone. The turreted roofs of the towers were rose pink and flowering vines covered the walls. It would have been breathtaking, but something horrible marred the beauty.

Attached to the castle was a great, black wart-like carbuncle that looked as if it had grown on the silver walls and rose-pink roofs.

'That's Night Witch work, Benbow,' Abby said to the great bird.

A long covered pier extended from the Night Witches' additions to the castle. It stretched out into the lake and there were walkways on each side. Extending from the roof was a massive chimney that stretched into the sky and appeared to reach as far as the roof of the dome.

Abby became aware of a loud, slow, monotonous chugging of machinery that was accompanied by a grumbling sigh. It sounded as if it came from the mouth of an angry giant. The sigh ended in a great booming thud that made the trees on the edge of the forest and the water of the lake tremble. There was a pause and the same sounds began to repeat themselves.

Abby could see no sign of life. Then, as Benbow flew in a widening circle above the castle, Abby spotted a place where a wide swathe of the forest had been cleared. Next to the clearing was an expanse of oily black water, dark as tar. A narrow stream of black liquid, which flowed from the Night Witches' extension to the castle, fed this second lake.

Suddenly there was the sound of a siren and Abby looked down to see Night Witches emerging from the building and running along the catwalks on each side of the pier. They were wearing black tight-fitting suits and some kind of breathing apparatus. Snout-like hoses ran from their face masks to tanks attached to their chests.

The surface of the lake began to foam and bubble and, with a whooshing sound, a black metal sphere burst to the surface and bobbed up and down close to the pier. The sphere was enormous. Abby judged there would be enough room inside to contain an elephant.

The Night Witches attached a grappling hook to it and winched it inside the covered pier.

Abby had seen enough. 'Let's go back to the Atlantis Boat, Benbow,' she called out, and he swung about to carry her towards the tunnel entrance.

Abby Discovers her Willpower

aptain Starlight was on the deck of the Atlantis Boat when Abby and Benbow returned. 'I see you remembered our position well enough,' he said as they landed.

'It wasn't too difficult,' Abby replied as she unfastened her harness. When she got below, Spike, Starlight and Sir Chadwick gathered around to hear her report.

'The suns are like giant insects in the sky, studded all over with tiny lights,' Abby began. 'And they use an airship to replace the bulbs,' she said.

'Yes, we saw that in the crystal ball as well,' Spike said.

Abby went on to tell them of the land inside the ice column. 'I think they are expecting some kind of bigger flying machine than the airship,' Abby said. 'Probably it's the one we saw inside the Night Witches' headquarters.'

She described the landing strip that had been cleared in the forest near the Night Witch fortress and the strange lake of black liquid.

Starlight nodded. 'Well, it looks as if our first problem is how to get inside the ice column.'

'It's heavily guarded,' Abby said.

'Maybe we could smuggle ourselves into one of the empty sledges on a return journey from the port,' Spike suggested.

'Sounds dangerous,' said Sir Chadwick. 'I think I shall consult Mandini.'

'But he's with the Sea Witch fleet, Sir Chadwick,' Abby said, worried that the strain was making him forgetful.

Sir Chadwick smiled. 'Forgive me,' he said, 'but I have to go into a trance for a minute or so.' He closed his eyes and held his hands to his head for a time, then he looked up and said, 'Mandini advises that we must capture their airship, overpower the crew and steal their uniforms. That would get two of us past the guards.'

'I didn't know you could do that – send thought messages,' said Spike, impressed.

'I wasn't sure I could,' said Sir Chadwick. Mandini only gave me the briefest of lessons. Of course, he is the greatest mind-reader of all the Light Witches.'

'How do we capture the airship?' Starlight asked.

Sir Chadwick gestured in the air. 'It services the artificial suns, doesn't it?'

'Yes.'

'If we bring one of the suns down, the airship will come to see what is wrong. Then we can overpower the crew.'

'A bold plan,' Starlight said, nodding in agreement.

'The airship has some kind of radio, I saw them talking into it,' Abby said.

'We'll have to capture them before they can get a message off.'

'How are we going to bring down one of the artificial suns?' asked Spike.

'Mandini suggested Light Witch Will.'

'Light Witch Will!' Abby repeated. 'How does that work?'

'It's a method we use to make a very powerful spell. It needs great concentration to generate the necessary energy,' said Sir Chadwick. He shrugged. 'The problem is, there's only me. It usually takes at least four Light Witches all holding hands.'

'What about Captain Starlight?' Abby said.

Starlight shook his head. 'Remember, I'm not a Light Witch, Abby.'

'Why not make Abby a member of the order?' said Spike. 'I bet she'd make a terrific Light Witch.'

Sir Chadwick considered the idea. 'She's very young.'

'But she's a smart girl,' Starlight said. 'She picked up the trick of vanishing in a trice.'

Sir Chadwick looked at him sternly. 'Strictly speaking, she shouldn't be doing that at all. You're not supposed to practise spells unless you're qualified.'

'Well, make her a member and it'll be all right, won't it?' persisted Spike.

Sir Chadwick was still reluctant. 'I studied for more

than a whole witch year before I qualified,' he grumbled. Then he held up his hands in surrender. 'But I suppose this *is* an emergency. I shall make her a provisional Light Witch.' He turned to Abby.

'Hold up your right hand and repeat after me: I promise to obey the laws of the Grand Order of Light Witches, pay my membership dues on the first of every month and obey the Grand Master on all matters of Light Witch policy.'

Abby repeated the oath. 'Is that all?' she asked.

'There's a five pound registration fee,' said Sir Chadwick. 'But under the circumstances we'll postpone payment.' He turned to Stardust. 'Now, I'll explain Mandini's plan in more detail.'

'First,' he said, 'Spike must keep an eye on the crystal ball to tell us when the airship is about.'

'Right,' said Spike. 'You can rely on me.'

'And you, Abby,' he said. 'I think it would be a good idea for you and I to practise Light Witch Will.'

He took her hands. 'First, we're going to make Spike rise in the air.'

'Are you?' Spike said, alarmed.

'Don't worry.' Sir Chadwick smiled reassuringly. 'It's quite harmless. You won't feel a thing. Just sit comfortably.' He turned back to Abby. 'What you have to do is imagine Spike rising about an arm's length from his seat. There must be no physical effort involved. Your imagination does all the work.'

Abby concentrated her mind on the image of Spike

rising and, sure enough, he gently floated up, still in the sitting position.

'Very good!' said Sir Chadwick, impressed. 'Now imagine lowering him down again.'

Spike fell with a thud. 'Hey,' he grumbled. 'I thought you said it was harmless?'

'Sorry, Spike,' said Abby. 'I won't do that again.'

'You won't get the chance,' said Spike.

'Nonetheless, your performance was excellent,' Sir Chadwick said with slight surprise. 'You clearly have an extraordinary natural ability, Abby. It takes some beginners a whole witch year to get it right.'

'Are you ready for something as big as the airship?' asked Spike, who had been watching the crystal ball. 'Because it's on its way.'

They looked at the ball and saw the fat black shape in the sky.

'Right,' said Starlight. 'I've got goggles for everyone, so we will be able to look at the suns. I'll take the boat to the embankment and put you ashore. I'll stand guard with my harpoon in case the serpent appears.'

A few minutes later, Abby stepped on to the river bank with Sir Chadwick. As they did so, she noticed their Atlantis capes immediately change from their usual blue colour to pure white.

Now all she could see of Sir Chadwick were his goggles.

Sir Chadwick took her hands and said, 'Concentrate on the nearest sun. Imagine it landing over there.' He nodded to a nearby rock.

Once more, Abby concentrated as Sir Chadwick had told her. Through her goggles she saw the artificial sun quiver for a moment, then gently curve through the sky like a falling star until it came to rest near the rock.

'It's working,' Spike called out from the boat. 'The airship has altered direction. It's heading this way.'

'Get ready to tackle the crew,' Starlight commanded.

'Where shall we hide?' said Spike who had joined Abby, Sir Chadwick and Starlight on the river bank.

'There's no need to. Just pull the hood of your Atlantis coat down over your head and you will blend into the background perfectly,' said Starlight.

'Are you going to use magic on them, Sir Chadwick?' asked Abby.

He shook his head. 'I want to save as much Ice Dust as I can,' he replied. 'Captain Starlight and I shall have to rely on old-fashioned fisticuffs.'

'It will be a pleasure,' said Starlight grimly.

Abby watched as the airship came closer. It circled the fallen sun once and then came down to hover a few feet from the ground. One of the crew leaped out and, taking a rope, tied it to an iron peg which he had quickly banged into the ground. The pilot joined him and they stood contemplating the fallen sun.

The problem clearly puzzled them because the wings that had held the machine aloft were continuing to beat. While the Night Witch crew stood nonplussed, Starlight and Sir Chadwick crept up and at the last second, Starlight gave his battle cry. 'Remember Bright Town!' he roared.

The crew of the airship spun round in astonishment, snatching for the wands they wore in scabbards at their waists. But Sir Chadwick and Starlight were quicker. Sir Chadwick hit the pilot with a left and then a right hook. He finished the job with a mighty uppercut that sent his opponent sprawling on the icy ground.

Captain Starlight's first blow struck the other crewman in his ample stomach, so that he doubled forward, making an 'oofing' sound as all the wind was driven from his body. Then, almost casually, Starlight raised his right fist and brought it down like a hammer on the back of the crewman's neck.

'Gosh,' said Spike in admiration. 'I'd like to be able to fight like that, wouldn't you, Abby?'

Abby didn't answer. She hadn't really enjoyed seeing the crew hurt, even though they were Night Witches.

Sir Chadwick now took the crewmen's wands in his finger tips and threw them into the river.

'What shall we do with them?' Starlight asked, waving at the unconcious foes.

'I should like to dump them in the river,' replied Sir Chadwick bitterly. 'But instead, I'll spare one speck of Ice Dust to put them to sleep for a fortnight.'

After removing the crewmen's helmets and flying coats, Starlight boarded the airship and examined the controls. 'Easy enough to fly,' he said after a few minutes.

'We'd better hide the machine in case the other Night Witches come looking for her,' Spike said. He pointed to the edge of a forest that was fairly close to where they stood. 'There looks enough space for you to park her between those trees. What do you think?'

'I could do that,' Starlight answered. But the machine is so black they still might spot it against the snow.'

'Why don't we spray her with water,' said Abby. 'Then the cold air will coat her with frost like everything else.'

'Excellent idea, Abby,' said Sir Chadwick. 'I congratulate you on your quick wits. We certainly are all making a splendid team.'

Starlight found a hose on board the boat and after a few minutes' work, the airship sparkled white like the surrounding countryside.

'Hold my hands, Abby,' said Sir Chadwick. 'We'd better get this sun back into the sky.'

No sooner had they completed the task, than they heard another droning noise. Suddenly, a great shadow passed across the snowy landscape. Abby and Spike looked up and started back in fear.

Low above their heads they saw what looked like a vast black insect moving slowly and menacingly in the direction of the fortress, leaving a long trail of oily black smoke in its wake.

'The new terror weapon Wolfbane boasted about,' Starlight said softly.

Suddenly, the radio in the airship crackled into life.

'Headquarters here,' said a tinny voice. 'You reported trouble with one of the suns.'

Sir Chadwick reached into the gondola and picked up the microphone. He held his nose to disguise his voice and replied. 'Airship to headquarters. We are making repairs.'

'Carry on,' the tinny voice answered.

'So it looks as if Wolfbane has arrived,' Sir Chadwick said. 'I smell more trouble.'

Benbow Brings News of the Night Witches

After they had eaten supper on board the boat, Captain Starlight called another conference. 'We have to get the Night Witch Shark Boats to set sail to attack the Light Witch fleet.'

'That shouldn't be too difficult,' Spike said. 'They seem to enjoy attacking things.'

Starlight nodded. 'Once they have sailed, I calculate we shall have twenty-four hours at the most.'

'To do what exactly?' asked Abby.

'Break into the Night Witch headquarters, free the prisoners, capture a large quantity of Ice Dust, and race to the Light Witch fleet to arm them before the Shark Boat fleet arrives to blow them all out of the water. A lot can go wrong,' Starlight said. 'We don't even know what goes on beneath the lake and in the Night Witch headquarters.'

'If only Spike could get his memory back,' said Abby.

Sir Chadwick stroked his chin. 'Maybe we can try an experiment with him,' he said. 'Your powers seem to be extraordinarily strong, Abby. It just might work.'

'What will you do to me?' asked Spike, remembering how they'd dropped him last time.

Sir Chadwick outlined his plan. 'Abby and I will hold hands with you and, through Light Witch Will, we shall enter one another's minds. Then I shall try to make contact with Mandini on the high seas. Perhaps his incredible abilities can unlock your memory, Spike.'

'Close your eyes and begin, now,' said Sir Chadwick.

'All think of a blue sky, Sir Chadwick intoned. 'No clouds, nothing but endless blueness.'

They did as instructed. Suddenly, a seagull flew across Abby's sky.'

'Whose bird was that?' Sir Chadwick asked.

'Mine,' said Spike. 'Sorry, it just slipped in.'

'That's all right,' said Sir Chadwick. 'Did you see it, Abby?'

'Yes,' she answered.

'Excellent,' said Sir Chadwick. 'Our minds are working together. 'Now I shall see if I can find Mandini.'

A moment later, Abby could see the Sea Witch fleet. It was as if she were standing on the pitching deck of a ship herself. Mandini's voice seemed to float into her mind.

'Hello, Abby, Spike, Sir Chadwick,' he said.

She heard Sir Chadwick reply in her mind. 'Mandini, I want you to probe Spike's mind to see if, by using our Light

Witch Will, you can unlock his memory.'

'It could be dangerous, Sir Chadwick,' Mandini said. 'I've never done this before. Suppose we all end up with each other's memories?'

'It's worth the risk.'

'As you wish, Master.'

Instantly, Abby began to see flickering images of places she had never seen before and faces of people she did not know.

'Keep thinking of the blue sky, Abby,' said Sir Chadwick.

Suddenly, Spike called out, 'Got it! I can remember what it is like inside the Night Witch fortress!'

'Just that? Nothing else?' asked Abby.

'Just that, but it's something,' said Spike.'

'Goodbye, Mandini. And well done,' said Sir Chadwick. Abby felt him let go of her hands.

'Tell us what goes on inside the ice column, Spike,' said Captain Starlight.

'The bottom of the lake is where the captured children harvested the Ice Dust,' Spike said

'So how does the process work?' asked Captain Starlight.

Spike continued, 'The Night Witches drop the big metal spheres with children in them to the bottom of the lake. The children swim out and harvest the Ice Dust. When they have enough, they blow out the water tanks and the sphere brings them back to the surface. Then the Night Witches take the sphere to the crusher.'

'What happens next?' asked Sir Chadwick.

'The Night Witches still can't go near it, so they have

other slaves to load the pure Ice Dust into the crusher.'

'What's the crusher?' said Abby.

Spike gestured with his hands. 'It's nothing but a massive hammer, really. The slaves load a combination of liquid toxic waste and Ice Dust on to a huge anvil. Then a large hammer comes down and crushes the mixture. The Ice Dust releases absolutely pure air, which is like a poison gas to the Night Witches. The pure air is sucked away through a great chimney. Oh, and a nasty stream of black liquid squirts out as well. All that remain are the blocks of Black Dust.'

'The black stream is what they're collecting in a new lake they've made outside the walls of the castle,' Abby said.

'Then what happens to the blocks of Black Dust?' asked Starlight.

'They are passed through an air lock to the Night Witches. They load them on to the sledges and take them to the port.'

Captain Starlight put his hand on Spike's shoulder. 'Can you remember yet how you escaped, Spike, or how you got the key to the Atlantis Boat?'

Spike shook his head. 'All I can recall is Abby's father telling me to find the Ancient Mariner and give him the key.'

'Where will the Light Witch fleet be now?' Sir Chadwick interrupted.

Captain Starlight did some calculations. While he was working at the chart table, Benbow suddenly appeared. He hopped over and put his beak close to Starlight's ear.

After a few moments, Starlight nodded and turned back

to the others. 'Important news. Benbow tells me the Night Witches know the Sea Witch fleet is on its way. It seems the Flying Insect spotted them on its way down here.'

'We must make haste,' said Sir Chadwick.

Starlight nodded grimly. 'Time is now critical, comrades. I'll send Benbow back to watch the Shark Boats. He'll tell us when they actually set sail. Then we'll make our next move.'

'What shall we do now?' Abby asked.

Starlight suddenly smiled. 'The best thing is to get some rest.'

'Isn't there something else I could do, Captain?' Spike asked.

'Me too,' said Abby. 'Just waiting is very difficult when you're anxious to get on with something.'

Sir Chadwick held up a hand. 'Captain Starlight is correct,' he said. 'I was a soldier once and we always tried to rest before a battle. When the Night Witches next switch off the suns, we'll get some sleep. We must be fit and refreshed for the struggle ahead.'

After they had eaten, Captain Starlight, who had been timing the periods of light and darkness, announced there was one minute before the suns went out. It took Abby some time to drift off because she kept remembering Starlight's words about the danger ahead.

When sleep finally came, she had a strange dream. She was in a great cavern where the floor was carpeted with glittering white dust. Vast stalagmites rose from the floor and stalactites hung from the roof. The rough walls were made of a silvery rock. Abby had seen it before. The castle by the lake was made of the same stone.

When she looked closer at the rock, she saw that it glittered with precious jewels. Far in the distance, she could see the glow of a blue light, and from that direction she could hear someone calling her.

She started to walk towards the light, quite unafraid. Then she woke up and, to her astonishment, she found she had been sleepwalking. She had wandered away from the Atlantis Boat and was standing on the edge of the river. Someone was still calling her name.

It was Captain Starlight.

Abby turned to retrace her steps but before she could call out, there was a splashing sound from the river and a

monstrous head reared up from the water. Abby had a moment to think it looked like a giant seahorse before the fearsome head darted forward and the terrifying creature swallowed her whole.

Spike Remembers All of His Past

A bby was astonished to find she was still alive inside the body of the beast. She began to struggle frantically, close to panic, striking out with her fists and feet. It was like punching and kicking a large sofa. She forced herself to become calm, and found she was far more comfortable than she could have expected to be. She could feel the monster's body all around her. But instead of being slimy, as she would have expected, it was quite dry and soft. More like upholstery, she thought. She couldn't move very much but she could breath quite easily.

Slowly, it dawned on her that the monster wasn't alive at all. It was some kind of mechanical contraption, and from the motion she could feel it was taking her somewhere at quite a speed.

'It's just another one of the Night Witches' machines,' she murmured. 'Strange this one doesn't smell. Well, they'll get a surprise when it spits me out, because I'll be invisible.' And she whistled her tune.

Abby could feel the great mechanical beast snaking through the water. After a time, it slowed down and finally stopped. The contraption immediately opened its mouth and ejected Abby. She was propelled forward into the light and for a moment she thought she was still asleep.

She was in the cavern she had dreamed of and the blue light illuminated a beautiful throne carved in pink rock and studded with polished jewels. A pretty girl dressed in a floating white dress sat upon it. She looked somehow familiar to Abby.

'Where are you, little girl?' she said sadly, tears brimming in her eyes. 'Oh, where are you? I'm so lonely.' Then she began to cry. Abby had heard that crying before, the night she and Benbow had slept in the forest.

The sound was so pitiful Abby felt sorry for her. 'Don't worry, I'm quite close,' Abby said.

'But I can't see you,' the girl answered, looking around in surprise.

Abby whistled her tune in reverse and reappeared.

'There you are,' said the girl, cheering up. 'How did you do that?'

'I'm not sure,' Abby replied. 'I just can. Who are you?'

The girl instantly regained her composure. She sat upright on her throne and now seemed rather haughty.

'I am Princess Galcia of Lantua. Who are you?'

'Abby Clover from the village of Speller.'

'Is that far away?'

'Very far.'

'I never go anywhere,' the princess said wistfully. 'I can't leave this cavern.'

'Why?'

'The ones called Night Witches would capture me like they did my brother.'

'Your brother?' Abby repeated. Then she gasped, 'Spike is your brother! You look just like him. That's why you look so familiar.'

'My brother is not called *Spike*,' the princess said proudly. 'His name is Altur, Prince of Lantua and all the Cold Seas. At least, he was before the Night ones did away with him.'

'You're wrong,' said Abby. 'They didn't do away with him. He's alive. We came here together.'

The princess shook her head. 'That's not possible. My serpent looked everywhere for him. That's how I know about you. My serpent saw you asleep in the forest.'

'I thought the serpent was a monstrous creature who ate people.'

Princess Galcia shook her head again. 'There was such a creature in the river long ago, but my ancestor, Turmec the Great, slew him. My serpent was made by the great ones who visited us in a magic boat. They gave it as a present to the royal children of the house of Turmec. It's thousands of years old.' She leaned forward and touched Abby's arm. 'But tell me more of Altur.'

'Your brother escaped, but he lost his memory. Now he has returned with my friends and me.'

'So Altur is still alive!' she cried excitedly. 'He must have swum away in the cold waters. Only he could do that. The other children would have frozen to death. So where is Altur now?'

'On our boat.'

'He will be in danger there. We must bring him here — where the Night ones cannot tread.'

'Why can't they come here?'

Princess Galcia pointed to the white dust on the floor. Abby looked about and saw that there were great heaps of it all about her.

'If they walk upon this they die.'

Abby looked down. 'Ice Dust,' she said. 'So much of it.'

She looked up at the princess. 'Why do you live down here? What happened to you?'

'Sit down, little girl,' the princess commanded, 'and I will tell you the story.'

Abby did as she was instructed and the princess began. 'Long, long ago, this was the land of Mordoc.'

'I've heard of him,' Abby said.

'Don't interrupt,' the princess said firmly. 'Mordoc was a wicked man. He enslaved the people who lived here. Then, one day, my noble ancestor, Turmec the Bold came in his long ship from far away in the north. He attacked Mordoc's fortress and defeated him. He freed the people and made a happy kingdom.

'But then, hundreds and hundreds of years ago, the fire mountains grew colder and the land froze. My ancestors continued to live on in the magic castle that Turmec had built. The last of our people stayed with them.'

'I've seen the castle,' said Abby.

The princess nodded. 'The magic lake keeps the land inside the ice column warm. My father, King Turmec IV was also a wise and kind ruler. But then, not long ago, the Night Witches came. They captured my mother, Queen Tayma, my father, King Turmec, and Prince Altur, and put them to work. They would have taken me as well but my father knew of this secret place. He just had time to hide me down here with my serpent.'

'What happened next?' asked Abby.

'The Night Witches began to steal the magic dust. They could not touch it themselves so they had to use others who they captured to do the work. They have terrible boats that sailed under the oceans to bring back slaves from across the seas as well. The prisoners could not escape because they could only swim in the warm waters of the lake. But Altur is different. He feels no cold. He must have swum along the cold river from the lake and out into the open sea.'

'He did,' Abby said. 'And a whale rescued him and brought him to where I live. If you come to the surface I can show you where he is.'

'What about my promise to my father not to leave?'

'I think your father would forgive you in the circum-stances, Your Highness,' Abby said. 'This is an emergency.'

'Very well,' the princess said. 'You may show me where

Prince Altur is.'

'Can we go back to where your serpent captured me?'

'The serpent will take us,' said Princess Galcia.

'We'd better hurry,' Abby replied.

Following the serpent, the princess and Abby hurried through the maze of tunnels. Abby noticed the walls were hung with a series of paintings that told a story. Abby studied them as the serpent led the way.

'Come on, little girl,' Princess Galcia called out, when Abby stopped momentarily to pay closer attention to the story the paintings were telling her.

'I'm coming,' Abby answered thoughtfully and hurried after the princess. After a time they came to a cave entrance where they stood in the gloom of the forest.

Abby could see they were quite near to the place where the Atlantis Boat was moored. Captain Starlight and Sir Chadwick were standing on the riverbank.

'Don't let them see the serpent until we have explained about it,' Abby said. 'They will think it's dangerous.'

Princess Galcia instructed the creature to wait, then Abby called out, 'I'm here.'

With shouts of relief, Sir Chadwick and Captain Starlight came to greet her.

'We thought you'd been eaten by the serpent,' said Starlight, looking relieved.

'I was,' said Abby, looking around. 'Where's Spike?'

'He's on watch at the crystal ball on the boat,' Sir Chadwick said. 'But who is this young lady?'

Abby turned to Princess Galcia. 'Forgive my bad manners, Your Highness. May I present Sir Chadwick Street and Captain Adam Starlight. Gentlemen... this is Princess Galcia.' The men bowed low.

Then Starlight spoke. 'Benbow reports that the Shark Boat fleet is preparing for sea as we speak. Spike is monitoring their movements. We'll never capture enough Ice Dust in time. The Sea Witch fleet will be destroyed.'

'But we do have time,' Abby said. 'There's masses of Ice Dust in the caverns beneath us. We can load it on to the airship and beat the Shark Boats if we hurry.'

Just then, Abby saw that Spike had come out of from the cabin on the boat.

'The Shark Boats look as if they're about to put to sea,' he called out — then he saw Princess Galcia and stopped in his tracks.

'Altur!' the princess cried joyfully. 'I thought I would never see you again.'

For a moment, Spike held a hand to his forehead. Then he rushed forward to hug her.

'Galcia!' he said. He stepped back, holding his head again, as thoughts raced through his brain. At last, he stood very straight. 'Now I know who I am!' He gestured to the others. 'And these are my friends.'

'What happened to you, Altur?' Galcia asked. 'What couldn't you remember?'

Spike held her hand. 'I was held captive with all the others. Our parents, Galcia, and yours, Abby, are among them.'

'Our parents had one hope. Abby's father still had the key to the Atlantis Boat. The Night Witches had taken everything else. Because I could swim in the cold waters, I was the only one who could escape so he gave the key to me.

'I swam from the lake into the river and out to sea. The Night Witches sent a Shark Boat after me. It ran me down and I was struck on the head. They thought I was dead, that I had perished in the great sea — but a whale found me and took me in his stomach to the town where Abby lived.'

'How did the whale know where to take you?' asked Abby.

'I told him to take me to the Ancient Mariner,' said Spike. 'That was all I could remember.'

'That explains it,' said Starlight. 'The whales knew I was going to Speller to look for the key to the Atlantis Boat.'

'How could you speak the language of whales, Spike — I mean Your Majesty?' Abby asked.

Spike smiled. 'I am Prince Altur, Lord of all the Cold Seas, I speak the language of penguins and seals as well. But you may continue to call me *Spike*, Abby.'

'And you may continue to call me *Abby*,' she replied, grinning. 'Otherwise I was going to insist on *Abigail*.'

Captain Starlight also smiled but was obviously becoming a trifle agitated.

'We must hurry and load the airship with Ice Dust,' he said.

'My serpent can do that,' Princess Galcia said, and she closed her eyes to concentrate. A few moments later the great mechanical creature slid towards them. Even though Abby knew it would not harm her, she still felt a small rush of fear at its awesome appearance.

'A truly terrifying device,' Sir Chadwick said with admiration. 'How I would like it to appear with me on the stage.'

'Where did it come from?' Starlight asked.

Princess Galcia held up an arm and the creature stopped before her. 'Long ago strange people who came from the stars visited our kingdom. They journeyed in a ship like yours,' she said, pointing to the Atlantis Boat. 'They made the serpent to amuse the children of the royal family. But the legend says that a real monster did once live in the river.' Then she addressed Starlight. 'Now, what task do you wish my serpent to perform?'

Starlight gestured towards the captured airship. 'Fill the cargo hold with Ice Dust, if you please, Your Highness.'

Princess Galcia clapped her hands and the creature snorted around at their feet for a few moments, then stuffed its nose into a hole in the ground.

'Stand back,' instructed Princess Galcia. They did as they were told and the creature gave a great intake of breath. Slowly it began to swell. Only when it was almost totally round did Princess Galcia hold up her hand for it to cease. The creature removed its nose from the hole and slid towards the airship.

Starlight had opened a cargo door and the serpent stuck its head into the space and slowly exhaled.

'Wonderful,' said Sir Chadwick, taking the opportunity

to recharge his wand. As he spoke, Benbow suddenly descended from the sky and whispered something to Starlight.

'We must hurry,' Starlight said. 'The Shark Boats are well underway.' Then he stopped. 'Who is going to fly the airship to the Sea Witch fleet?'

Sir Chadwick waved a hand. 'If you set the controls on automatic, I shall contact Mandini and he will use the power of his mind to bring it to him without us needing a pilot aboard.'

While Starlight made adjustments in the cockpit, Sir Chadwick let his thoughts go to the Sea Witch fleet.

'Mandini says, "We shall fight to the last cannon ball",' said Sir Chadwick, as the airship zoomed above them.

They watched until it was out of sight, then Captain Starlight said, 'Now all we have to do is attack the fortress and rescue the prisoners.'

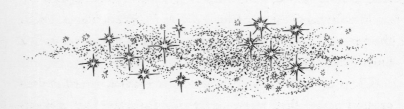

Captain Starlight's Plan of Attack

'Now that Spike's memory has been restored he can tell us more about the Night Witch fortress,' Starlight said when they had gathered below on the Atlantis Boat.

Spike looked somehow more important to Abby as he stood before them. She could easily imagine him dressed as a prince.

'The heart of the Kingdom of Lantua is the Lake of Life,' he began. 'The water is quite pure. At the bottom is a small volcano. That is why the water is always warm. From the volcano comes a stream of liquid fire that turns to Ice Dust when it meets the water.

'Beneath Lantua, there was once a great maze of underground lakes that were fed from fissures in the rocks beneath the Lake of Life. My ancestors sealed the fissures to the underground lakes and they gradually dried out, leaving the caverns as a place of refuge and the great deposits of Ice Dust. And that is where Abby found my sister, Galcia.'

'What about the river?' Sir Chadwick asked.

Spike turned to him. 'My ancestors did not attempt to seal up the river.'

'Can we get the Atlantis Boat through it and into the lake?' Starlight asked.

Spike answered, 'No, the crack is too narrow for the boat, and it twists and turns.'

'My serpent might get through,' Princess Galcia volunteered.

'Yes, I think it might just be able to. But it would be a very tight squeeze,' said Spike.

Starlight nodded. 'Go on.'

'When the Night Witches came, they built their fortress on to the castle. First they made the great machines to crush the Ice Dust, then they brought more captives and the black sludge to mix with it.'

'Where do they hold the captives?' Sir Chadwick asked.

Spike continued. 'The base of the Night Witch fortress is the old castle courtyard. It serves both as a slave camp and a factory. That is where the prisoners are, and where they keep the great machines that crush the Ice Dust.

'Where are my parents?' Abby asked.

'They were with mine,' Spike answered. 'Working the crushers that hammer the goodness out of the Ice Dust.'

'Why don't they just collect the Ice Dust in the underground caverns?' Sir Chadwick asked.

'The Night Witches still don't know about the underground caverns. That is why my parents hid Galcia in them.'

Starlight thought for a time. Then he spoke to Spike. 'Why don't the grown-ups try to escape?' he asked.

'It's impossible. As the river gets close to the sea it becomes too cold for them. They would freeze to death. Cold water does not bother me.'

'Couldn't the grown-ups fight the guards?' asked Sir Chadwick.

Spike shook his head again. 'It would be pointless. They could never cross the Wall of Evil.'

'What's that?'

Spike held up his hands. 'It's hard to explain. There is some strange black fog inside the castle wall that surrounds the factory and dungeons. Go near it and it fills you with terror the moment you approach. No one except the Night Witches can cross it.'

Starlight turned to Sir Chadwick. 'What do you think that could be?'

Sir Chadwick pursed his lips. 'Hard to say. I know of a Night Witch spell that can fill a room with fear, but I've never encountered a *wall* of fear. It must be something new they have made with Black Dust.'

'Do you think you could make a hole in it?'

'Possibly, but from what Spike says there must be masses of people in there. I would be fighting the Night Witch guards at the same time. I couldn't guarantee everyone escaping.'

'How many of the Night Witch guards do we think are left at the fortress, Spike?' asked Starlight.

'We saw most of them in the crystal, going off to sail with the Shark Boat fleet,' Spike said. 'But there's about half a dozen still in the fortress with Wolfbane and the troll guards.'

Starlight sat and thought for a long time. Then he stood up and spoke to Sir Chadwick. 'Can you make a spell with Ice Dust that would allow the serpent to blow a hole in the Wall of Fear?'

Sir Chadwick nodded. 'That should be possible.'

'Good,' said Starlight. 'And we still have the uniforms we took from the Night Witches in the airship?'

'Yes,' Abby answered.

'Right, this is the plan. Princess Galcia, Spike and Abby will enter the Lake of Life inside the serpent. It is going to be a tight squeeze because the serpent must also carry a charge of Ice Dust that Sir Chadwick will have worked a spell on.'

Starlight looked to Princess Galcia. 'Will the serpent be able to carry you all and a large charge of Ice Dust?'

She thought for a moment. 'Yes, it will, Captain.'

Starlight lay a hand on Spike's shoulder. 'Just exactly where is the main gate to the fortress?'

'I'll show you in the crystal,' Spike said, and he concentrated until a picture of two great doors bound with brass, appeared in the ball.

Starlight turned to Abby, Spike and Galcia. 'When you three have entered the slave camp you must make your way to the point nearest these gates. I'm afraid you won't have time for lengthy reunions with your parents. In fact, it would be best if Abby makes you all invisible.'

'I understand,' said Abby.

'When you get to the Wall of Fear, the serpent must use some of the Ice Dust that Sir Chadwick has treated to blow a gap. You go through and open the gates. Sir Chadwick and I will be on the other side, disguised as Night Witches.'

'What about the Atlantis Boat?' asked Abby.

'We shall bring it as far as we can then leave it on the riverbed.'

'Then what happens?' asked Spike.

'Once through the gate to the fortress we shall be out-numbered, but we shall have the element of surprise on our side. So it will be up to Sir Chadwick and myself to defeat them.'

'And us,' chorused Abby, Spike and Galcia.

Sir Chadwick stood up and clapped Starlight on the shoulder. 'A capital plan, Sir. Simple, bold and clever. Mandini couldn't have done better. I take my hat off to you.'

'Now we shall wait for the darkness,' Starlight said.

The Children of
the Lake

When the artificial suns were darkened once again, Princess Galcia led them to the caverns beneath the earth. They were all astonished by the great caves, but Sir Chadwick was almost overcome by the sight of the thick carpet of Ice Dust that sparkled beneath their feet. 'Enough for a millennium,' he sighed.

'And the lake keeps making more,' Spike reminded him.

'Quick now,' Captain Starlight said urgently. 'We need to know how much space will be left for Ice Dust once the three children are inside the serpent.'

Galcia watched as Captain Starlight and Sir Chadwick heaped Ice Dust at her feet. When she judged it was the amount they could take inside the serpent, she held up her hand.

Sir Chadwick began to chant over the precious pile until it glowed in different colours and then returned to a shining white.

Captain Starlight handed Abby his gold pocket watch. 'We shall be outside the gate of the fortress at twelve o'clock,' he said. 'That's when you must break through the Wall of Fear and let us in.'

Abby put the watch carefully into her pocket.

'Good luck,' said Sir Chadwick and Captain Starlight together.

Once the three children were seated inside the serpent, Princess Galcia said, 'If you feel above your head you will find some goggles. Put them on and you will be able to see where we are going, just as if you were looking through the eyes of the serpent. Now, if everyone is ready, we'll go.'

The creature slid forward and, once again, Abby felt the strange wriggling motion, but this time she could see where they were going. After a few minutes they came to the river-bank and the serpent slipped into the water.

Abby could see the Atlantis Boat resting on the bottom as they glided past and began to journey upstream. Gradually, the river-bed became more tangled with weeds.

'It's because the water is getting warmer,' Spike explained.

They watched as strange, almost transparent, fish flashed by and curious, crab-like creatures lurked on the river-bed. Abby was comfortable in the stomach of the serpent and was so fascinated by the changing river she quite forgot the passing time, until Spike said, 'The current is stronger now. We are getting close to the entrance to the lake.'

The weeds in the river were bending to the flow, then a great craggy wall of pink stone loomed up before them. It had a long jagged crack in its face.

'This is going to be a tight squeeze,' Spike called out.

The serpent began to writhe from side to side as it slid through the narrow crack.

For one heart-stopping moment, Abby thought they were going to get stuck, but the serpent eased its way through and they emerged in the Lake of Life.

The water was a beautiful blue, the colour of cornflowers, and crystal clear. Abby could see the floor of the lake sparkling with Ice Dust. Shoals of fish swam by. They were no longer transparent but glowed with all the colours of the rainbow. In the centre of the lake was a mount, the tip shining with a bright blue light. Clouds of Ice Dust swirled around it.

'The volcano,' said Spike.

Through the clear water they could see that, far away, the bed of the lake was studded with black metal spheres and children were swimming about them, gathering Ice Dust. They hadn't noticed the serpent's arrival.

'Stop the serpent, Galcia,' Spike called out and as the creature slowly came to rest on the bed of the lake, he added, 'we'll wait here. A sphere will come down close to us soon enough.'

'What shall we do then?' Abby asked.

'I'll swim over to the child and explain what we're going to do.'

'How do the children breath under water?' asked Abby.

'They don't,' said Spike. 'Only those who can hold their breath for a long time are chosen for this job. The Night Witches thought if they gave us breathing equipment we might find a way out.'

'The sphere I saw was pretty big,' said Abby. 'It must take a long time to fill it up.'

'It does,' said Spike. 'It takes hundreds of trips, going back and forth to fill your lungs again. You get very tired.'

Abby continued to watch the rainbow-coloured shoals of passing fish while they waited. After a time, as Spike predicted, one of the huge black metal spheres began to descend through the clear water and came to rest close to them on the bed of the lake. A hatch opened in the side and a girl swam from the sphere.

She wore a swimming costume made of rags and carried a large shoulder bag. She began to fill it by scooping up Ice Dust from the lake bed with a trowel. The girl did not notice the serpent which had almost buried itself in the thick layer of Ice Dust on the bed of the lake.

'That's Claris, I remember her,' Spike said excitedly. 'I'm going out to talk.'

Spike swam out through the mouth of the serpent and when he came close to the girl she looked up, startled. Abby and Galcia watched as he communicated with the girl in sign language. After a few moments, the girl returned to the sphere and Spike swam back and gestured for Galcia and Abby to follow him. Abby took a deep breath and followed Galcia out through the mouth of the serpent.

Spike gestured for them to enter the sphere, and as they passed through its air lock, they faced Spike and the girl in a gloomy interior. Spike introduced Abby and Galcia to the girl and said, 'We've come to rescue you all, Claris.'

The girl shook her head sadly. 'That's impossible. How can children defeat the Night Witches?'

'We have powerful friends,' Spike continued. 'But we will need your help.'

'To do what?'

'Instead of filling this sphere with Ice Dust, we want you to smuggle us and our serpent into the Night Witch fortress.'

'Serpent!' Claris exclaimed. 'What serpent?'

'Don't worry,' Galcia reassured her. 'It's only a toy. It won't hurt you.'

Abby looked around them. 'It'll be quite a crush in here.'

Spike nodded. 'Don't worry, there'll be a little more space when we blow the water ballast to get us back to the surface.' He spoke to the girl again. 'We'll have to stay down here for a while so they think you've gathered a full load. Will you help us, Claris?'

'Of course, Altur. It's wonderful to see you again. We all tried to guess what happened to you when you escaped.'

'I had all sorts of adventures. Then a whale took me to Speller where I met Abby.'

Claris looked at Abby thoughtfully, then said, 'I know you. Your family runs the town shop. You were very small when I last saw you.'

'You're from Speller!' Abby said, astonished.

'Most of the children in the fortress are,' Claris replied. 'The Night Witches stole us to work here.'

'Do you know my parents? Are they safe?'

Claris shook her head. 'I don't know. The Night Witches took them away yesterday. We haven't seen them since.'

'What about my parents?' Galcia asked.

Claris turned to her. 'They took the king and queen as well. We don't know what they did with them.'

'Yesterday!' Abby repeated bitterly. 'They were in the fortress until yesterday.' Then she saw that Galcia was near to tears and she took her hand. 'Cheer up Galcia,' she said bravely. 'I'm sure they'll be safe.'

But she wasn't sure in her heart.

'We'd better get the serpent on board,' Spike said after a moment of silence. He swam from the sphere again and returned with the creature. It took them ages to get it inside.

'Right,' said Spike eventually. 'I think we can go up now. We'd better make ourselves invisible, Abby. We'll make Claris invisible too.'

'Why?' Claris asked.

'When they open the sphere, the Night Witches on the observation platform will think it's empty. If we hold hands until we're clear of them you can slip away.'

'Won't the Night Witches be suspicious of an empty sphere?' asked Abby.

Spike shook his head. 'It often happens. Children become exhausted. The others rescue them and take them into their own spheres. Then they send up the empty one. The Night Witches will just think Claris is still below.'

Spike looked around. 'I think we've waited long enough, Claris. Press the bell and blow the tanks.'

Claris did as Spike instructed and he explained to Galcia and Abby that the bell would warn the Night Witches that a sphere was coming up.

They could all feel the sphere rising. Through a tiny porthole, Abby watched the other children still working on the lake bed below. After a few seconds they were bobbing up and down on the surface. There was the scraping sound of the hook being attached and they felt the sphere swing free of the water.

'Not long now,' Spike said in a tight voice, 'and we'll be inside the fortress.'

'Will we feel anything as we pass through the Wall of Fear?' Galcia asked.

'No,' Claris told them. 'The metal of the sphere is too thick.'

The swaying sensation continued for a time, then there were a few bumps and the sphere came to a halt.

'They will be uncoupling us now,' Claris explained. 'Any moment now, the whole top of the sphere will open so they can remove the Ice Dust.'

'Everyone hold hands. Galcia, hold the serpent's ear,' Abby said.

'How exciting,' Claris said. 'I've never been invisible before.'

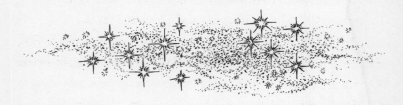

The Battle on
the Staircase

When the top half of the sphere swung open inside the slave camp, a group of ragged children, holding shovels in their hands, stood looking into the seemingly empty sphere.

'Quick now,' Abby called out, and the children started back, astonished by a voice that seemed to come out of thin air. Holding hands, Abby, Claris, Spike, and Galcia, who clasped the ear of the serpent, scrambled from the sphere to stand in the fortress courtyard.

Abby glanced at Captain Starlight's gold watch, it was ten minutes to twelve o'clock. They had to get a move on. Abby looked about her. At first, the sheer size of the compound they stood in came as a surprise. It was a vast area, made grim and gloomy by the swirling black foggy boundaries of the Wall of Fear.

The old, white stone floor was covered with a greasy black coating and, rising above the Wall of Fear, was a complex of iron galleries and observation posts, from which Night Witches looked down.

In the centre of the courtyard there was a great mass of gigantic, black-painted machines that produced the deafening noises made by the steady beat of the crushing hammers. Grouped about them was a dismal shanty town of shacks where Abby imagined the captives must live.

Supported on high gantries, two lines of metal containers swung from overhead tracks which converged at the mighty hammers. One line of containers held vats of black oily liquid, the other the Ice Dust unloaded from the spheres.

Groups of children were heaving the containers to mix the two ingredients together in vats that were pushed into place. When the vast hammers smashed down on the mixture, a great hood descended for a moment and there was a loud sucking sound. After the concussive blow, a thin black liquid gushed into a channel cut into the stone floor where it sloped away from the machines.

When the hammers rose again, children reached into the anvils and extracted blocks of black material that were the size of house bricks.

'Black Dust,' Spike shouted over the sound of the machines. 'Now you see how they make it.'

Abby glanced towards the Night Witches looking down from the observation platform. When she judged the moment was right, she said. 'Quick, Claris. All clear, join the other children.'

Claris let go of her hand and, visible again, slipped in

among the other children all around them who were tending the machines. There was a loading bay where the raw toxic liquid was poured into the containers. Others sat on a line of benches, heads bowed, waiting to take their place in the spheres and be returned to the lake.

The stench from the liquid containers was worse than anything Abby had ever smelt before. It was so strong that every breath she took almost choked her.

This is a terrible place, she thought, worse than any nightmare.

Spike nudged her and pointed up above the metal galleries to the nearest observation platform where two Night Witches in protection suits patrolled.

'They don't suspect anything. This way to the gate,' Spike shouted and, still holding hands to keep them invisible, they made their way in the direction Spike indicated.

As they crossed the greasy stone floor and passed under the tangle of girders that supported the galleries, Abby could see the Wall of Fear more clearly. At first glance it looked like a dense black cloud of smoke. But writhing demons and fearsome beasts were trapped in its darkness. Abby began to feel a terrible sensation of unhappiness and revulsion. She wanted to turn away but she knew they must press on. Finally, they could go no further.

The swirling black wall was only inches away from them and the demons and snakes seemed to be reaching out to lure them into the evil mist. Spike was looking about him, desperately trying to gain his bearings and locate exactly where the gates lay beyond the threatening fog.

'Hurry, Altur,' cried Galcia. 'I can't stand this awful feeling much longer.'

'Here!' called Spike, pointing to the Wall of Fear. 'Let the serpent make the breach just here, Galcia,' he shouted.

As he called out, Abby suddenly slipped on the greasy floor. She let go of Spike's hand and immediately the others reappeared. A siren screamed. Glancing up at the observation gallery, Abby saw the Night Witches pointing down at them as Galcia directed the serpent to aim a stream of Ice Dust at the Wall of Fear.

At first, it seemed to make no impression but, gradually, the menacing cloud began to shrivel and a ragged hole appeared. Through it they could see a wide concourse and, beyond it, the fortress gates set in the high walls of the old castle. Following Spike's lead, they all tumbled through.

After a moment of startled surprise, the trolls guarding

the gates began running towards them. But the serpent slid forward and shot forth another stream of Ice Dust.

It was as if the trolls had suddenly been forced back by a jet of scalding water. They tore at their protective clothes before collapsing into a twitching, writhing heap.

Abby looked at Starlight's watch: one minute to twelve o'clock.

'Quick, the gates!' she shouted and they all ran forward. There were two great wheels which raised the huge bars locking the gate. They seized them and attempted to haul them around. They tried with all their might but they couldn't budge those wheels at all!

'Use some magic on them, Abby,' Spike shouted.

'But I don't know any magic,' she shouted back.

'Try anything,' said Galcia. 'But *hurry!*'

Abby looked up desperately and shouted,

> 'Open quick
> Or I'll be sick!'

To her amazement, the wheels they clutched began to turn smoothly.

They could hear shouting outside and when the gates finally swung open they saw Captain Starlight and Sir Chadwick fighting fiercely with six of the troll guards. Starlight was using his harpoon like a great pike and Sir Chadwick wielded his wand like a rapier.

'Stand aside,' Galcia shouted.

Starlight and Sir Chadwick jumped back as the serpent shot a long stream of Ice Dust over their adversaries.

Abby quickly looked about her. To their right was a great wide curving flight of steps that passed above the confines of the slave camp. Each step was flanked with statues of demons and snakelike creatures. Far, far away, at the head of the staircase, were two more mighty doors leading in to the castle.

'This way,' she shouted as Starlight dispatched the last of the trolls with a sweep of his harpoon. Abby, Spike, Galcia, Sir Chadwick and Starlight all dashed towards the great flight of stairs. As they raced up, Abby saw Benbow flying above them.

On and on they ran, up the massive curving staircase. Below them, the captive children stared up through the murky gloom.

As they approached the top of the staircase there was a thunderous booming sound as the mighty gates at the top opened. A column of trolls, armed with pikes, paused for a moment, then began to march down the staircase, their long boots crashing on every step.

'Apart from pikes do they have any other kind of weapon, Spike?' Starlight asked, not taking his eyes off the descending column of trolls.

Spike shook his head. 'No, the Night Witches won't trust them with anything but whips and pikes in case they're tempted to rise up.'

Captain Starlight held up an arm. 'Sir Chadwick and I will stand on either side of the serpent,' he commanded. 'The rest of you take your places behind. Princess Galcia, be so kind as to direct the fire of the serpent where you think fit.'

Slowly, they advanced to meet the massed ranks of trolls.

When the enemy was almost upon them, Galcia gave the order to fire and the serpent blew a withering path through their ranks. Sir Chadwick and Captain Starlight rushed forward to engage with those who had escaped the blast.

The battle raged all around Abby and for a time she thought they might be overwhelmed. She and Spike picked up pikes from fallen trolls and threw them at the attackers, while Galcia, quite coolly in spite of the danger, directed her serpent's fire.

The fighting was fierce but, gradually, Sir Chadwick and Starlight, aided by the children and the serpent, won through. Trolls had fallen all about them and, finally, with the last puff of Ice Dust left in its body the serpent blew away the last of the enemy. Galcia leaned forward and whispered in the serpent's ear. 'You can do no more, my friend. Hide yourself until I call for you again,' and she watched as the creature slithered down the staircase.

Sir Chadwick and Captain Starlight stood for a moment among the heaps of groaning trolls that were sprawled all down the staircase. Sir Chadwick held out his wand and shook it gently. One last shining particle of Ice Dust flew from the point. It was the same for Captain Starlight. The blade of his harpoon had lost it polished gleam and the glint had gone from its cutting edges.

'Come on,' Starlight called out wearily. 'It's nearly finished.' They pressed forward to cross the threshold beyond the great doors.

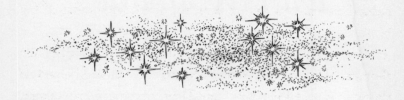

Face to Face
with Wolfbane

'This was my father's throne room but it never looked like this,' Spike said as they entered a vast hall paved with greasy black flagstones. The walls and ceiling were entirely covered in ugly iron spikes, like the hide of a giant porcupine. In the centre of the hall was a solitary throne where the Chief of the Night Witches sat, coldly watching them.

'Your time is finished, evil one,' Sir Chadwick's rich voice boomed.

The hideous figure studied them as they grew closer. He was smiling.

'As usual, Chadwick, you are quite wrong,' he said in a relaxed manner. 'Actually, my time is just beginning.'

He raised a hand and gave a languid wave. A row of the spikes that studded the ceiling thudded down to pierce the stone floor like giant arrows, narrowly missing Abby and her companions.

As Starlight and Sir Chadwick were about to attack

Wolfbane, he laughed hideously. 'Move, and next time they will pierce your bodies,' he shouted.

Starlight and Sir Chadwick drew back and Wolfbane continued, 'Prince Altur, how nice to see you again. And you have been thoughtful enough to bring me your sister as well.'

He reached down beside the throne and picked up a black object that looked rather like an old fashioned camera with a long lens. 'This is my latest device – the Atomizer. You may have seen an earlier prototype. We have now perfected it. Let me show you what it does.'

Wolfbane lay the device down next to the throne and took something from the folds of his cloak. 'I suppose you and your sister want to see your parents again? Well, here they are.' With that, he threw down two tiny crystal cubes.

'I'm afraid I had to atomize them, but don't worry – it is a fate that might quite soon come to you all.' Wolfbane gazed at them smugly. His expression changed as a thought flickered across his mind. 'And where is the other child from Speller?' he said, producing two more crystals. 'I have her parents here as well.' And he threw them down at their feet.

Abby could see they too contained the minute figures of a man and a woman.

Abby wanted to fly at Wolfbane but she knew it was important for her to remain undetected. Instead, while Wolfbane looked away, she silently took all the cubes from the floor and put them in her pocket. Spike and Galcia saw all the cubes vanish but said nothing.

'Abby is quite safe, Wolfbane,' Sir Chadwick said with as much conviction as he could pretend to muster. 'At this moment she is on her way to help destroy your Shark Boats.'

The Chief of Night Witches laughed harshly. 'So now you call me by my proper name instead of Cheeseman?'

Sir Chadwick shrugged. 'It suits you — cheese is something delicious and useful. Wolfbane is poisonous — just like you.'

The Chief of Night Witches smiled. 'I'm sorry I've missed your little friend from Speller but I will see her soon. Once I have concluded our business here, I shall destroy her and the Sea Witch fleet for ever.'

'Not as long as I have breath in my body,' Sir Chadwick said defiantly.

Wolfbane sniggered. 'I could arrange that! In fact, breathless will be your permanent state quite soon. But before that, I have one more pleasurable diversion for you to perform.'

Wolfbane looked over his shoulder at the sound of marching feet. 'If I am not mistaken,' he continued, 'that is my personal bodyguard. They are armed, and their weapons fully charged with Black Dust. And yours are exhausted — a pity.' The bodyguard of Night Witches halted next to the throne.

'Seize Galcia and Altur!' Wolfbane ordered. 'If these two men give you any trouble cut the little dears' royal throats.'

Captain Starlight and Sir Chadwick exchanged glances, shrugged and lay down their weapons.

'Good,' Wolfbane said. 'Now, if you will all be kind enough to follow me.'

He swept from the throne and walked ahead of the procession.

Abby slipped silently to one side until she was alone in the gloomy hall. When they were out of earshot she called out softly, 'Benbow.'

The great bird swooped down from above, where he had been hiding.

'Take me after them,' Abby whispered as she seized Benbow's legs.

Abby Remembers
a Special Secret

Benbow and Abby soon caught up and hovered above the procession as Wolfbane continued his boastful monologue. 'I suppose, Prince Altur and Princess Galcia, you can hardly recognise the old palace since I made all these improvements,' he said as they came out on to the battlements of the castle walls. He pointed at the gigantic, ugly, black additions that had been built on to the pink stone.

'It looks like a giant wart on a beautiful face,' Sir Chadwick growled.

'Ah!' said Wolfbane, 'but you must have heard the expression, *beauty is in the eye of the beholder*? To me, it looks quite exquisite. But soon you shall see my real masterpiece.'

He led them down successive flights of stairs and into what had once been a glorious garden. Now, it was overgrown and wasted. They passed through the remains of an orchard where all the fruit was withering on the branches.

The sluggish river of black oily liquid bubbled from the earth by the castle wall.

Wolfbane continued to lead them along a muddy path beside the black stream which smelt as dreadful as the inside of the captives' camp.

The party approached the edge of the forest, where the stream fed into the lake of black liquid. The path lead to a landing stage, which reached out almost to the centre of the lake. Wolfbane led the group to the end of the promenade and turned to address them. He gestured around him and said. 'I understand you are familiar with the history of my kingdom?'

'We know enough,' Sir Chadwick replied.

Wolfbane held up his hand again. 'Then let me tell you of my latest addition. You will recall the legend that there was once a terrible serpent living in the river?'

'Yes.'

'Well, the legend was true. My servants found its bones when they were building my additions to the castle.' He drew himself up proudly.

'With the new power of Black Dust – behold what I have done!'

He seized Galcia by her shoulders and thrust her forward to the very edge of the landing stage.

There was a gurgling sound from the black lake and the surface erupted. The head of a vast slimy creature rose up from the depths. It was shaped like Galcia's serpent but was twice as big and infinitely more terrifying.

'I have remade the creature!' Wolfbane cried out in triumph.

Courageous as they were, even Captain Starlight and Sir Chadwick drew back a step at the monstrous sight. 'Dear heavens, it truly is a creature from hell,' Sir Chadwick gasped.

Looking down from where she and Benbow hovered, Abby saw the serpent darting its hideous head from side to side. It rose even further out of the black lake and Abby noticed something else. The fearsome creature seemed to be in some kind of agonising pain. She could make out great wounds on its body, where the heads of ancient spears and arrows were embedded in its flesh.

Wolfbane turned his head to address his Night Witch guards. 'Hand these gentlemen their weapons and throw them to my creature.' The guards handed Captain Starlight his dull-bladed harpoon and Sir Chadwick his empty wand. The two men shrugged off the guards and Sir Chadwick raised his wand in a flourishing salute. 'Farewell, children,' he called out, 'I'm so sorry we failed.'

'Good luck, Sir Chadwick, Captain Starlight,' the three children replied.

Sir Chadwick turned to Captain Starlight and gave a slight bow. 'I could not wish to die in better company, Ancient Mariner.'

'Nor I, Master of Light Witches,' Starlight replied, and with his battle cry on his lips, he leaped with Sir Chadwick into the black water.

The monster gave a roaring bellow and darted its head

towards Sir Chadwick, who drove his wand into its neck. The creature wrenched away and the wand was plucked from Sir Chadwick's hand.

Captain Starlight raised his harpoon and threw it with all his might. The blade sunk into the creature's body. The serpent turned its head and seized the visible part of the harpoon in its mouth and broke it off, leaving the blade buried in its weeping flesh. Then it gave a great squealing cry and with incredible speed made two snapping motions and gulped Sir Chadwick and then Captain Starlight into its vast mouth.

Wolfbane laughed with delight. 'Goodbye, Sir Chadwick. I wonder if I shall miss you in the centuries to come?' Then he turned to Spike and Galcia. 'Now, I'm afraid the good times are over. It is time for you to join your companions in the slave camp. But it won't be for long. Soon you will be playthings for my Night Witches.'

Abby felt her heart was about to burst with grief. She had grown to love Captain Starlight and Sir Chadwick. It did not seem possible they could be gone. Helpless, all she could do was weep. She wanted to fight Wolfbane herself and, although she had no weapon, she was about to attack him. But, through her tears, she suddenly remembered something important.

'Take me down, Benbow,' she said softly.

Wolfbane had turned away after the creature sunk back into the lake. Abby landed in front of him and whistled her tune in reverse. He looked startled by her sudden appearance – but almost instantly recovered.

'Starlight's little friend, I presume,' he said. 'How kind of you to surrender.'

'You are an evil old beast, Wolfbane,' Abby said, unafraid. 'Your creature cannot harm me.'

'Well, we shall see,' said Wolfbane. Still holding Galcia, he raised one arm to summon the serpent again.

Once more it rose with a roar from the bed of the lake. Abby stood calmly at the end of the landing stage.

'Run, Abby, run!' Spike called to her, struggling with one of the Night Witch guards.

But Abby stood her ground as the vast slimy head hovered before her, bellowing with hateful rage.

Wolfbane cackled with delight at its anger but stopped when he saw Abby hold out a hand.

'Poor, poor creature,' she said softly. 'People have been very unkind to you, haven't they?' The head of the beast stopped swaying and it looked into Abby's eyes for a long time. 'I know what you have suffered,' Abby continued. 'I promise I won't hurt you.'

The creature continued to stare at Abby and then, to Spike and Galcia's amazement, tears began to trickle down its slime-blackened cheeks.

'Stop, stop,' Wolfbane cried out, pushing forward in sudden alarm. 'What are you doing to my monster?'

At Wolfbane's words the creature turned its head and made a snapping motion in his direction. He darted out of its reach just in time.

The creature now lay its head down on the landing stage

and Abby reached forward and began to pull out the blades and arrowheads of the ancient weapons that were embedded in its body.

Spike and Galcia watched in silence now. With each weapon Abby removed from the creature's hide, its body became paler and paler. The slime slid away and gradually the serpent began to glow a soft golden colour.

Wolfbane stared in horror as, with a great hiccuping sound, the creature suddenly opened its mouth and, after a mighty belch, ejected Captain Starlight and Sir Chadwick on to the landing stage. They were still alive!

Starlight was the first to his feet. 'Kindness!' he said when he recovered his voice. 'The Atlantis Boat told us the creature could not fight kindness.'

As the transformation of the serpent continued, the black liquid of the lake began to turn to pure blue water.

'What is happening?' Galcia said, confused by the sudden turn of events.

The serpent began to speak in the language of the Seven Seas and Spike translated. 'I had lived in the Lake of Life for a millennium before Mordoc came. I had no evil in my heart until then. But Mordoc cast a spell upon me,' said the serpent. 'I was supposed to live for all eternity in pain. Men came to fight me and they only added to my agony. That is why I was feared.' He now reached out and nuzzled Abby with his great head. 'This child has ended my pain and by her kindness has made me good once more.' Then he turned with a roar. 'But it is now your time to suffer,

Wolfbane!' The creature heaved itself from the now clear waters of the lake and began to slide towards the Chief of the Night Witches.

'No, no!' Wolfbane screamed in terror and scuttled off towards the edge of the forest, his bodyguard at his side.

'Look,' Galcia called out and they turned to see yet another transformation taking place. The river of black liquid flowing from the fortress had also turned to pure blue water and, as it reached the castle, great lumps of the Night Witches' warty additions began to fall away from the original structure.

'It looks as if the Lake of Life is destroying all the vile work done by the Night Witches,' Starlight said in wonder.

Sir Chadwick suddenly seized his arm. 'Quick, Starlight. Remember the children's parents. We must use the Atomizer to reverse the process before it is also destroyed.'

Filled with a new fear, they all ran back towards the castle. Breathlessly, they climbed flights of stairs and raced through corridors and passageways until they reached the hall where Wolfbane had placed the contraption next to the throne.

Sir Chadwick snatched up the Atomizer and examined it quickly. 'I can't see any way of reversing the process,' he said. 'There's just this compartment for Black Dust.'

'Suppose we put Ice Dust in it instead?' Spike suggested.

'It's worth a try,' Sir Chadwick answered grimly.

The whole building was now shaking as if they were in an

earthquake. More of the Night Witches' additions began to tumble away and the air was full of choking dust and the sounds of crashing masonry and distant rumblings. The iron spikes began to fall from the ceiling and walls to reveal a great window through which they could see the Lake of Life.

'How can we get some Ice Dust?' Sir Chadwick shouted above the noise.

'Benbow,' Starlight called out. 'Bring us Ice Dust from the bed of the lake.' Benbow gave a loud squawk and flew through the window. They watched as he rose high into the air before closing his wings and diving like an arrow into the depths of the water. Abby held her breath, until he rose again and flew back to the hall.

'Put it in here,' said Starlight, pointing to the compartment in the machine. Hovering above them, Benbow released enough of the Ice Dust to fill the Atomizer.

'Let's hope it works,' said Sir Chadwick as they placed all the tiny crystal cubes Abby had taken from her pocket on to the trembling floor.

Sir Chadwick aimed the machine and it began to shake and splutter. There was a loud sizzling sound and a sudden jet of Ice Dust covered the crystals. 'Stand back,' Sir Chadwick warned.

The crystals began to quiver and then, with a succession of bangs, grew larger and larger. The process was reversed!

Suddenly, standing before them, and looking slightly bewildered, were the King and Queen of Lantua and Abby's parents. And so were Sally Oak and the polar bear.

They all looked distinctly dazed, especially the polar bear.

Despite the shaking of the room, the children rushed to embrace their parents, all of them laughing and crying at the same time.

Sir Chadwick interrupted urgently, 'If Your Majesties and ladies and gentlemen will allow, I think we should all seek safer ground.'

The polar bear still looked baffled, but Spike spoke a few words to him in the language of the Seven Seas and he followed him quite happily.

Sir Chadwick hurried them to the great staircase where they had fought their battle.

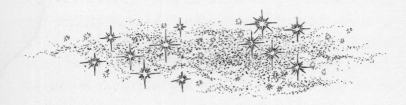

Fighting the Shark Boat Fleet

*I*n the courtyard below, there was growing jubilation as the transformation continued. The Wall of Fear had dissolved completely and the trolls had fled. The warty additions the Night Witches had made to the castle were crumbling away and the ground had ceased its quaking.

The captive children now stood in ragged groups amid the newly revealed splendours of the old castle.

Sir Chadwick addressed them. 'Children,' he called out. 'You are all free. The Night Witches are defeated and have fled. Quite soon we will restore you to your parents. You have nothing more to fear.'

No sooner had he stopped speaking than there was a droning sound and Abby looked up to see Wolfbane's giant insect machine passing overhead.

Starlight looked suddenly anxious. 'Wolfbane has escaped and they still have weapons aboard.'

'Heading for the Sea Witch fleet, no doubt,' Sir Chadwick said grimly.

'What can we do?' Abby asked.

Sir Chadwick cupped his hands to his mouth and shouted: 'Children, you are the sons and daughters of Sea Witches. Hold hands with Abby, Sally Oak and me and help us use the power of Light Witch Will to bring down that flying machine.'

'How do we do that?' a child near Abby called out.

'Imagine you are forcing the flying machine to come down by pressing a big weight on it,' Sally Oak answered. 'Tell the others.'

'Hold hands, all together, *now!*' Sir Chadwick commanded.

The flying machine continued to glide towards the tunnel in the column of ice. But then it began to wobble as if a giant hand were pressing down on its back. Slowly, it sank lower and lower until it rested at the edge of the forest.

'Quick now,' commanded Starlight. 'Surround it.'

The children, led by Abby and Spike, ran to the flying machine and stood with snowballs of Ice Dust at the ready. The doors burst open and the Night Witch bodyguard charged from the machine, brandishing their weapons.

Before they could fire they were met by a barrage of Ice Dust balls flung by the army of angry children. Made helpless by the power of the Ice Dust, the Night Witches dropped their weapons and began to claw frantically at their own faces and clothes.

'Enough!' cried out Sir Chadwick, finally.

The children drew back, leaving the huddled figures of

the bodyguard moaning and whimpering on the ground.

Starlight and Sir Chadwick quickly inspected the Night Witches. 'There's no sign of Wolfbane,' Sir Chadwick said. 'He's tricked us! The flying machine was merely a diversion. He must have used some other escape route.'

'Too late to worry,' Sir Chadwick answered. 'Sally Oak, help their majesties to take charge here. The rest of us, on to the flying machine. We can use it to help Mandini fight the Shark Boat fleet.'

But the King of Lantua shook his head and turned to the other adults who had also been held captive. 'My people, we are near to victory. Now my family and I must take part in the last battle. The young lady called Sally Oak will help you care for the captive children. We shall return soon.'

Spike, Abby, Galcia, Benbow, Starlight and Sir Chadwick, with Abby's parents and the King and Queen, all scrambled aboard the flying insect.

Inside were gun ports armed with Atomizers, and a great cargo area filled with sinister black bombs. Starlight inspected the controls. 'I can fly this machine,' he said, 'but what about all the weapons?'

'Keep the Atomizers, we'll load them with Ice Dust. Dump the bombs into the Lake of Life,' Sir Chadwick answered. 'Its power will easily destroy them.'

'Ready now,' Starlight shouted. 'I'm going to take off.'

'Wait,' called Galcia. 'I can see the serpents coming.'

Abby looked from a gunport and saw both the creatures

weaving towards them. Galcia opened the hatch again and
they slid up the ramp, both looking very fat.

Abby was about to ask why, when the machine lurched
into the air. They paused only to dump the Night Witches'
bombs into the lake, then Starlight steered the machine
towards the tunnel in the column of ice.

Once they were clear of the dome and over the ocean,
Captain Starlight took the machine up to full speed and
they raced across the water.

'Will we be in time?' Abby asked anxiously.

Starlight glanced at his watch, which Abby had returned
to him. 'It's going to be pretty close,' he replied grimly.

Suddenly, Sir Chadwick slapped his hand to his head. 'Ice Dust!' he gasped in dismay. 'In our haste we forgot to load up with Ice Dust.'

'No, we didn't,' said Galcia. 'The serpents filled themselves with it.'

Sir Chadwick sat back with a sigh of relief. 'Arm the Atomizers with Ice Dust,' he instructed the crew.

Despite the danger they still faced, Abby and Spike looked about them happily as their parents worked alongside them, preparing for battle. Galcia was now in charge of the two serpents and directed them to where the Ice Dust was needed.

'All ready, Captain Starlight,' Sir Chadwick said when all the Atomizers were fully loaded.

The machine began to quiver as Captain Starlight slowed her down. 'The Sea Witch fleet is dead ahead,' he announced from the cockpit. 'And the battle is underway.'

Abby, Spike and Galcia were looking through the same gun port at the scene below. It was obvious that things were not going too well for the Sea Witch fleet. At least half of the ships had masts missing and others floated helplessly in a tangle of wreckage. All were scattered over a wide area of sea, some almost as far away as the horizon.

Dozens of Shark Boats and submarines were circling the Sea Witch ships like packs of hungry wolves, blasting with their guns and firing shoals of torpedoes into the sailing ships.

Occasionally, a broadside of cannon balls from a Sea Witch ship would strike home and a Shark Boat or submarine would explode with a belch of oily black smoke, but the Night Witches were clearly winning.

'I can't make out what the trouble is with our ships,' Starlight said grimly.

'Nor I,' answered Sir Chadwick. 'We'd better stay out of range until we understand the situation.'

'Can't you contact Mandini in your mind, Sir Chadwick?' asked Spike.

Sir Chadwick shook his head. 'He's concentrating too hard on the battle at the moment.'

'I'll get Benbow to take me down so I can and ask him what we should do to help,' Abby said.

'Take care, darling,' her mother called anxiously.

Seizing hold of Benbow's legs, Abby whistled her tune. Spike opened a hatch and they soared out of the machine.

Benbow circled the fleet once. Spotting Mandini standing on the quarterdeck of Mr Halyard's schooner, he landed beside him.

'Fire at the submarine that has just surfaced,' Mandini yelled out, and there was a thunderous crash as the crew discharged a broadside of canon balls. Then he saw Abby. 'Where did you spring from, my dear?' he asked coolly.

'We've captured the Night Witch flying machine,' she replied, ducking as a shell whistled overhead. She glanced along the length of the schooner and saw Hilda bandaging a wounded seaman next to one of the cannons. 'Captain Starlight and Sir Chadwick want to know what the situation is,' Abby shouted above the sound of the explosions.

Mandini did not take his eyes from the battle. 'Shortage of Ice Dust,' he answered. 'We had to use most of our supply to bring the Shark Boat submarines to the surface. Now we don't have enough to finish them off. In fact they're giving us a serious beating.' He turned and shouted, 'Bring her into the wind – we must help that sailing barge that's in trouble.'

Abby looked about her. 'Why do you have the Sea Witch fleet so scattered?' she asked.

'If we all grouped together they could form one big wolf pack, concentrate their gunfire and torpedoes in one spot and wipe us out.'

'If you do bring them all together I know a way we can beat them,' Abby said.

Mandini looked away from the battle and wiped a gunpowder stain from his forehead. 'It's too risky, child,' he answered as the rail he stood next to was blown away by a

Night Witch shell which narrowly missed them.

'I don't have time to explain, Mandini. *Please* just trust me,' Abby said.

Mandini paused, removed his hat with an exaggerated flourish and bowed deeply. 'I trust you, Abby. I shall gather the Sea Witch fleet as you wish.' He turned and shouted to his yeoman. 'Make a signal. All ships rally to me – close as you can.' Then he added to Abby. 'That will bring the Shark Boats down on us in one pack for sure.'

'Thank you,' Abby answered. 'You really are a great man.' She called out to Benbow and grabbed his legs. 'Back to the flying machine, Benbow,' she commanded.

When they reached the hovering machine, Benbow flew them through the open hatch. Spike and his parents, the King and Queen of Lantua and Sir Chadwick were firing all their atomizers down at the Shark Boats. Galcia was keeping them loaded with Ice Dust. Some of the Shark Boats below were returning their fire. Whistling her tune in reverse, Abby raced over to Starlight.

'Mandini is calling the fleet together in close formation. That will cause the Shark Boats to cluster into one tight pack as well.'

Starlight and Sir Chadwick immediately understood what she had done. 'I'll take the machine down,' Starlight shouted. 'Galcia, when we're above the Shark Boats send out the serpents.'

Through the gun port, Abby could see that Mandini's action was beginning to bring about the effect she had intended. As the Sea Witch fleet gathered in a tight circle, the Shark Boats also began to form a great pack.

Suddenly, the flying insect was hit by one of the Shark Boat shells. It blew a great gaping hole in the body and a piece of the flying debris struck Abby a glancing blow on the head, stunning Benbow at the same time. The machine lurched for a moment and Abby fell through the hole blown in the side.

As the rest of the crew were still concentrating their fire on the Shark Boats, only Spike saw her tumbling through the air. There was a small splash near the Shark Boats as she sank beneath the waves.

Spike did not hesitate. He dived after her, through the gaping hole blown by the shell.

Unconscious, Abby sank deeper and deeper into the cold ocean. She came to for a moment, and felt the shock of the icy cold water on her face. The rest of her was quite warm because she still wore her Atlantis cape. It seemed quite peaceful as she continued to sink into the darkness.

She felt herself suddenly grasped roughly around the waist. She stopped sinking and realised she was being hauled back to the surface. As the sea grew brighter, she saw Spike, legs moving like pistons desperately fighting to save them both.

They broke to the surface and found themselves in the middle of the Shark Boat pack. Captain Starlight was beside them now, after jumping in himself, clutching his harpoon and swimming with all his might. Abby felt groggy, but heard Starlight shouting out, 'Get her away, Spike,' as two Shark Boats bore down on them.

Spike struck out and Captain Starlight turned on the Shark Boat, his harpoon thrust out before him. Spike and Abby were well clear when they heard a shattering boom behind them and the smell of the destroyed Shark Boat drifted over them.

Above, Sir Chadwick, who had taken over the controls from Starlight, aimed the flying machine at the great concentration of Shark Boats and flew at full speed towards them. When they were just above the surface of the ocean, he called out, 'Galcia, release the serpents.'

'Go!' Galcia shouted when they were almost on the Shark Boat pack.

The two serpents dived from the machine into the sea and... disappeared.

The Shark Boats were lining up to fire a final salvo of torpedoes at the helpless Sea Witch ships.

'Oh, no! Where are the serpents?' gasped Abby's father.

'Look! There!' called Abby's mother as the serpents surfaced behind the Night Witch fleet.

'Now!' Galcia yelled. Both serpents raised their mighty heads and blew a vast billowing cloud of Ice Dust over the ranks of Shark Boats.

As if some giant hand had sprinkled the sinister black shapes with icing sugar, the Shark Boat fleet gleamed white in the bright sunlight. But not for long. The ships began to crack open with a succession of shattering bangs. At every explosion, a dark cloud of oily smoke belched up and the Shark Boats were suddenly sucked down beneath the waves.

'Hang on,' Sir Chadwick called out as the flying machine wobbled violently, 'I think we are about to crash.'

The Night Witch flying machine skipped across the waves briefly before coming to rest on the surface of the sea.

Great cheers went up from the Sea Witch fleet and they quickly steered in close to the machine to rescue its passengers.

Abby and Spike were hauled aboard and immediately rushed to the side to look anxiously for Captain Starlight. Benbow saw him first and hovered protectively above his head as he swam to the rescue boat.

The Victory Ball

*A*bby would always remember it as the happiest day of her life. At last, she could hug her mother and father properly as they stood on the quarterdeck of Mandini's flagship.

The serpents, sensing the importance of the occasion, swam about the fleet of ships, blowing fabulous fountains of seawater into the sky. Benbow flew overhead, squawking his approval.

'I always knew I'd find you again,' Abby said to her parents, as she stood between them, squeezing their hands.

'We've missed you so much,' Abby's mother said, brushing a tear from her cheek. 'And now we shall be able to see you every day.'

'Every day,' Abby repeated and it didn't seem possible to her that she could be so happy.

After a time, Spike left his own family and walked towards Abby. He looked both the same but also very different. He bowed elegantly to Abby's father and said, 'His Majesty, my father, King Turmec IV of Lantua and Ruler of the Cold Seas, commands me to invite you to a Grand Ball of Celebration in the Palace of Lantua tomorrow evening.'

Abby's mother was flustered for a moment and looked down at the rags she still wore. 'That's very gracious of His Majesty,' she replied. Then she turned to her husband. 'But I haven't got a thing to wear.' Abby laughed and took a pinch of Ice Dust from her pocket. She sprinkled it over her mother. Her ragged clothes glowed for a moment, then were transformed into a dazzling silk ball-gown.

Spike was about to go on but stopped suddenly, 'Abby,' he said. 'How did you remember to treat the serpent with kindness? I had forgotten what the Atlantis Boat told us.'

'It was in the caves where Galcia was hiding,' Abby replied. 'The real truth about the serpent was in the paintings on the walls. They had been done by the original people of Lantua who had lived on the island even before Mordoc came. So I knew it had been transformed by Mordoc from being a kind creature into a monster.'

Spike thought for a moment. 'We haven't found Wolfbane yet. I wonder if we'll ever see him again?'

Sir Chadwick overheard Spike from where he was standing with Hilda. 'Bad pennies have a way of turning up,' he said. 'We shall have to keep an eye open for him in the future.'

Spike turned to Mandini. 'Admiral,' he said, 'would you make a signal to the fleet, inviting everyone to the Grand Ball tomorrow night?'

'Of course, Your Highness,' Mandini replied. 'But I

don't actually have the title of Admiral, you know.'

'You shall be promoted at the ball,' Spike replied.

It wasn't just Mandini who was decorated the following evening. After the feasting and dancing, King Turmec announced that Sir Chadwick had been made a Duke of Lantua and Abby would, henceforth, hold the title of Duchess of the Cold Seas, which she thought was pretty grand for a young girl.

The only person missing was Captain Starlight. No one had seen him or Benbow since they had returned to the castle. Mandini checked and reported that there was no sign of the Atlantis Boat either.

Abby was sad that she hadn't had a chance to say good-bye, but her father consoled her. 'Adam Starlight never did like a fuss,' he said. 'Don't worry, Abby. One day, when you least expect it, he'll turn up again.'

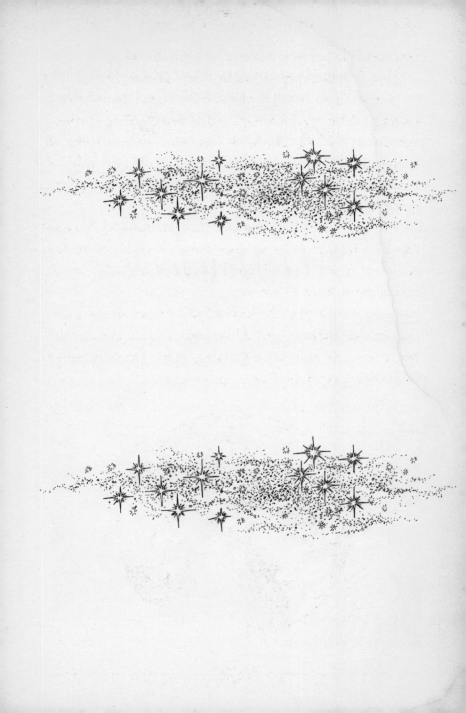

Read more about Abby, Benbow and friends in The Time Witches *to be published in Autumn 2002. Once again Wolfbane has hatched up an evil plan — to travel back in time and defeat Abby and the Light Witches by changing the past!*

Here is an extract from The Time Witches . . .

Raising the Spirit of Ma Hemlock

The dreadful creature that froze Sid Rollin to his chair was a massive black and yellow spider. It crouched in the flickering candlelight, framed by the open window. Its body was the size of a cat but its hairy

legs spread across the entire width of the windowsill. The spider paused for a moment before leaping on to the table in front of Wolfbane.

'Mr Rollin,' Wolfbane purred with satisfaction. 'Let me introduce you to Baal, my familiar.'

'Your familiar?' Rollin repeated faintly.

Wolfbane nodded. 'It's a term used for the creatures we Night Witches have as pets and assistants. Legend has it that they are always black cats. As you see, that is not so.'

'How did it get so big?' Rollin asked, curious despite his horror.

Wolfbane smiled and gestured with his cigar. 'I owe that to my mother. She supplied me with the necessary potion, I merely boosted its performance with something of my own. Here, you see the result.'

Sid Rollin recovered slightly. He began to rise slowly from his seat. Wolfbane gestured again with his cigar. 'Baal,' he commanded. 'Secure him.'

With startling speed, the gigantic spider spun a glistening cord from its body, looped it about Sid Rollin's shoulders and bound him to his chair.

Wolfbane sat back in his seat with satisfaction. 'Now, Baal, tell me what you have discovered about my enemies.'

The spider drew close to its master and began to whisper in his ear.

'First class,' said Wolfbane after a time. 'And you actually visited the lighthouse and saw the documents Abby

Clover's parents have gathered?' The spider continued to whisper and Wolfbane nodded in satisfaction.

'So, now I know, Jack Elvin is the key to it all,' he exclaimed finally. 'If I remove him from history my problems will vanish like melted snow.'